Coming Of Age

JD Whisperling

ISBN:
ISBN-13: 978-0615483399

DEDICATION

To my loving siblings and few family members who have walked with me in life, loved me for who I am, inspired me to live my life to the fullest with no regrets, I dedicate this book to you, with all my love in return.

Joe

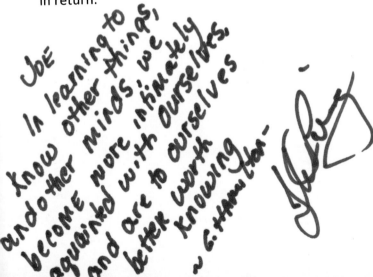

In learning to know other things, and other minds, we become more intimately aquainted with ourselves, and are to ourselves better worth knowing
~ G. Hamilton

[illegible]

Joe,
In learning to
know other things, we
know other minds, inevitably
become more acquainted with ourselves
and are better to know
others. –

INTRODUCTION

I It started as any other day would, getting dressed in clothing outdated and revolting to the fashion world, washing my face making sure not to be wasteful of water, while listening to gospel being preached on the radio. Then off to the kitchen to eat a mundane, bland bowl of oatmeal, with scant portions allowed, and a miniscule allotment of milk to cool it, and barely disguising its close resemblance to a pasty substance used to spackle a wall. Yet it was breakfast and I was hungry from missing my evening meal the night before as a punishment for my sinful behavior. Just an ordinary day in our house was beginning. One couldn't fathom calling it a home, with its calloused environment filled with disdain, for what seemed to be, every thought or worldly wish I held within me. Little did I know that today of all days, unknown to me, the future, would forever be changed.

We were told sternly to get into the car, "time was of the essence and we were running late", my mother curtly shouted. When I heard her tone, as usual, my sister and I fled to the car, hastened by the imminent fear that non compliance would be reciprocated with a paddling of our behinds on barren cheeks with a wooden paddle so commonly referred to as the *board of correction, to be applied to the seat of learning*. An experience we lived often, in pain, and tears, knowing deep within that it not only brought us into submission, but a hate for even residing in such a cruel existence.

We sat there whispering amongst each other in the back seat of the car about our lessons and homework, not paying much mind to where we were headed as we knew the trek to the private religious school we were forced to attend, to separate ourselves from the *common sinners doomed for hell*, was a 45 minute commute we did every weekday. Something seemed different; the radio was not blaring Christian music, my mother was unusually silent, with a stern and cross look of deep concentration on her face, I then looked up and noticed at that moment we were not heading in the direction of the school, but towards my grandmother's house. Perhaps school was cancelled, and we were not informed? A day at grandma and grandpa's house was always filled with warmth and love. This was much better than school.

We rushed from the car into the arms of grandma waiting at the door. She embraced me in her arms and told me she loved me, repeatedly giving me kisses and hugging me tightly. She always had a warm embrace, a warm heart and loving arms to wrap around us. But this time it seemed a bit odd, she held on much tighter and longer and repeated over and over, "I love you", as if she were saying good-bye. Within moments I would realize, to me, she was saying good-bye.

I started to take my coat off and my mother informed me that I needed to keep it on, she was taking me to a girls home where I could be isolated from the sin I was choosing to do, and I could be taught the errors of my ways through strict discipline and reform. She told me she had packed a few of my clothes the night before and had not spoken of her intent to prevent me from running away to my father's home. He was of Satan, because he had chosen a life of sin and worldliness, and I must not turn out like him. My heart sank, I felt as if someone had just drained the life out of me as if I were a used tire with a defective valve, flat and unusable. What could I have done so horrible, to be sent away? All I wanted was to have what every other kid in our neighborhood had. Even though my mother referred to them as sinners and people that were of Satan's will, I did not see evil horns upon their head, nor a miserable existence. It was true I rebelled, in a juvenile attempt to make my mother see that we, our family were the ones with the existence that seemed strange and unordinary, not everyone else. I cried, silently, afraid.

-1-

The two day drive, with few stops and no chance to wash my face or eat anything besides drive-thru rubbish, ended with the car going down a winding clay and dirt road and arriving in a small back woods private community area in Louisiana. I could read a broken down sign that bore a name barely legible and a scripture passage underneath *'The Lord knows the way of the righteous, but the way of the ungodly shall perish'*.

We passed a few trailer houses as we made our way to the sign perched on a bent pole, that said "Office", and stopped in a gravel parking space and my mother opened her door and stretched. She then motioned for me to get out of the car, I did. By now I was trembling. She told me, 'stay put and do not move', and like a lap dog awaiting a treat, I did. My mind and eyes however did not, they were taking in everything around me. I saw rundown buildings in need of fresh paint, fencing that was taller than me topped with barbed wire surrounding the whole exterior of the mock village and a few wooden fences separating a few outbuildings. All the buildings had numbers in red painted above the doors, and dangling from the open door bars were chains and padlocks, some rusted from exposure to the elements.

I was not quite sure at first what to think. Had I fallen asleep and awakened in some alternate universe? What was this man made hell hole? I closed my eyes for a moment, and said to myself, 'please wake up, please, don't let this be real'. I opened my eyes, and about that time a breeze hit me, and reality dictated I was screwed. The heat was sweltering, the humidity felt as if one needed a brush hog to clear a path to move, and there was a stench in the air that made me want so badly, to lean over the back of the car and just hurl my guts out. Later I would learn quickly where that repugnant odor that filled the ozone had originated.

In the distance I could see girls carrying buckets and gardening tools, barefoot, and worn, some stumbling, some crying, being escorted in a straight line walking along the fence, with a large burly woman carrying a stick walking along them hitting those that whimpered or complained. My concentration on the girls and what they were complaining about was brought to a halt when my mother reappeared from the building, with a tall fat man in a cowboy hat, carrying a large family bible, and abruptly said to me, “the devil will lose control of you once and for all”.

I was told to follow him into the building to get settled in my new abode. I thought to myself that if I complied nicely and did not fight, the man would see perhaps my mother was wrong and I was a good girl and not the spawn of Satan she thought I was and he would tell me I should be taken back home. Another one of those juvenile misconceptions! Upon entering the door, I was ushered by 2 women one way, as my mother and the man, I later found out to be named, *Brother Mack*, went inside an office and shut the door.

The ladies, although they do not by any means deserve that title, proceeded to grab my clothes and pull them from me and strip me naked. I grabbed desperately at my clothing as it was being ripped from me, crying and begging them to let me undress myself, as they slapped and spat at me telling me I was a vile sinner and must be cleansed. My head started to swim, the room was spinning, I felt faint, as I began to hear chanting around me and a circle of girls gathered and collected my clothes from the floor and I was ushered into a shower to be scrubbed.

The water was very cold, and smelled of sulfur and was a yellow tint as from an old cistern unmaintained, yet was soothing to the welts from repeated blows upon my body. The two ladies then reached into the shower and commenced to cleansing the bad spirits within, with harsh words and degrading comments as they proceeded. I felt violated as strange hands engulfed my body with scrub brushes and soap that reeked like floor cleaner. I sighed in relief when they finished, hoping perhaps this was just an initiation process, and truly not an everyday occurrence. I will never forget the feeling of being violated during a strip search full cavity probe before I had even had the chance to reach full chronological womanhood. Now really who would dare 'stash' ungodly items there?

I was then given an ugly gray plaid dress, granny panties 3 sizes too big, and an old tattered bra with safety pins to put on, and told I must wear that until they check my things brought by my mother, in case I had brought something that would entice sin upon myself and bring shame to God. Where the hell were the fashion police! Sometimes the things my mother forced me to wear were hideous, but this outfit went far beyond that, this was just a violation of visual rights to wear something that would not bring an urge to vomit should they look in the mirror. Good thing there were no mirrors, or I would have thrown up just seeing myself.

I asked for a pair of shoes to put on. That was a mistake. No sooner had I uttered the request, when I felt a sting so painful it had brought me to my knees. I had never been hit so hard in the face in my life! I grasped my cheek, and could feel blood running from my lip, as I fell to the floor, my face to the tile, crying and begging to myself, 'God, please don't make me stay here, I promise to be good'. I was abruptly pulled to my feet and told by the lady who called herself *Sister Ruth,* that I must never speak without being spoken to, I shall never ask for something other than life as I am not deserving of even that, and it was time for me to sit down and learn the rules that I must memorize and be able to quote before the week's end.

There I sat in a rusted metal folding chair with an old stained table, corners taped with duct tape and old carved initials scratched out, in front of me and a few papers neatly stacked upon it, that I was to read and memorize. Across the table sat Sister Ruth and a girl close to my age, both with Bibles in hand and a look of hate that could have seared a hole clean through me like a hot poker for a fireplace could sear thru a tissue. A lump formed in my throat, as I battled whether to cry, or scream, and I found I was too numb to do either.

To this day I still remember the rules, as if engrained inside of my brain like an ill gotten tattoo applied in a drunken haze. They were as follows:

- No one speaks until spoken to (for me, an opinionated person, this was not a good thing).
- There will be no utterance of anything worldly such as radio or television shows.

- There will be no singing or humming of any songs, except ones taught there or in the church hymnals.
- There will be no pictures of any kind. One must never write anything except a letter home once a month (of course we were told what we were to write).
- There will be no idle time. When one is not working they must be in prayer or reading and memorizing the scriptures.
- One must always look at the floor as we are all shameful sinners, unless speaking to a Brother or Sister in charge.
- If we see someone sinning and do not report it we will receive their punishment with them.
- If we have unchristian thoughts we must repent them to a Sister or Brother immediately for rebuking.
- We must go nowhere alone.

- We must follow all dormitory rules without complaint.
- We must do everything Brother Mack says, as he is God's Chosen One to spread his message.

I thought to myself, this was going to be a very long stay. Dormitory rules? What other rules could be as bad as these? No Radio. No television. No Newspapers. No Visitors. No Freedom of Speech. No talking about anything unrelated to God or the Bible. No unauthorized information from the outside world? No jokes, no laughter, no looking anywhere but directly into the back of the head of the person standing in front of us when in line or at the floor. For until my spirit and will were *right with God;* I was considered unworthy to view anything else?

You must spend idle time in prayer and silence, Surely this would be a task that would be hard for me to accomplish. Idle time was something I would also find out later, did not exist. I must urinate, shower, dress, and anything else in the presence of one of the assigned "big sisters' that would help guide the "demons' of Satan from within me. Yes, it was true, I had arrived and started taking up residence in Hell, Louisiana!

Sister Ruth asked me if I had any questions about anything, I had the one opportunity to ask, and then I was to leave my life behind and start anew as a follower of the "True Believer's Way". I should have kept my mouth shut, but anyone that knows me now, knows that is not possible. I asked her, "what did I do that was so bad to deserve this"? Bad Idea.

Before I could even blink, that crazed ass bitch came from around the table snatched me up by my hair, and proceeded to bend me over the table, still clutching my hair tightly and repeatedly smack my butt with her hand as the young gal started to read aloud the accusations of my sinful ways brought to their attention by my mother. She began to read aloud.. *You looked upon a boy with lust in your eyes inappropriately; you lied to your mother about where you were as you partook in worldly actions with sinners; you stole items which did not belong to you; you defiled a church with poor conduct; you did not obey the rules that your mother demanded of you.....* she continued reading, but at this point the swatting was starting to sting so badly, I was in tears, gasping, crying and I could no longer make sense of the words and just screamed, "yes, I am sorry". Then she let go of my hair and pushed me down onto the chair to sit and they left the room, locking the door behind them. I felt as if I was sitting on a bed of hot coals, my butt now throbbing, I felt as if death would have been a better option. Not something that usually crosses the mind of someone as young as I was, but so relevant and so real to my wants at that moment.

I lifted my skirt too peer at the wounds inflicted upon me quickly before they returned, my cheeks swollen and a hue of blood was risen to the surface making it look as if my butt were a tomato that had just been blanched.

I laid my arms on the table then rested my head on them, replaying in my mind the accusations and what it was I actually did that led me to be such a horrible child that I would do these unspeakable acts. I was guilty as charged. I knew I had looked at a boy at school after my mother had told me not to. But the boy was charming and always nice to me. His name was Mitch, he was my brother's friend, and always had something nice to say to me the few times he was close enough to speak to me. He would wave after school from the parking lot as we would drive away. I was a girl after all and it is just common curiosity to reciprocate an interest and a hello and chat, is that not what all kids do? I saw other's do it at the Church and school we went to. Why was I so different? What was the harm in having a friend that was a boy?

Oh yes, I remember now! Because boys are evil! It will start with talk, then lust, then kissing then sin. When I look back in time, I now think my mother's disdain for the opposite sex may have been her lack of being able to have a productive relationship with any male, and she had to not allow us the privilege in retaliation for what was lacking in her social abilities.

I too had lied and stolen. I had lied to my mother about where I was on many occasions. She worked two jobs and was gone often. We were supposed to stay at home and do chores or work to help pay for our room and board, as nothing in life is free. But I had chosen on many occasions to sneak away and play amongst the neighbor kids, and lied about it, then got caught.

I stole food when I was hungry because the food we ate was not enough rations to feed one person and was frequently divvied amongst 3 of us kids. Do you really think it is unjust to steal food for survival? Many a day my mother would feast on a large meal in front of us, as we were given mere morsels, barely enough to stimulate the appetite, let alone sustain us above the level of malnutrition. I even once stole some things and hid them just to try and purposely be kicked out of a school we attended because I hated the punishments and rules enforced on us.

There is nothing more miserable than having ideals and religion crammed down your throat so much you feel even farting will send you to hell. As to the accusation of defiling a church, I am not sure what was meant by that, but in my youthful revolt against the religious Reich I was forced to endure, I am sure by their laws I did that too. Shit, I was a kid after all, we are entitled to a few misgivings, before we are plummeted into a living hell aren't we? Perhaps not in my case, I did often find myself revolting against my mother's brutal upbringing of us by going against as many of her rules as I could in hopes that she would just give me away. Once again, those misguided juvenile thoughts ran awry. Now don't get me wrong. I don't feel that God, religion and good discipline is a bad thing at all, but when you're forced into compliance to the point you lose your own individuality and identity, and beaten for not complying, then it becomes a problem. We spent countless hours reading from scriptures, listening to gospel radio programs, attending revivals and religious themed outings while others spent their family time watching movies, playing sports, and hanging out with others in the neighborhood. How much does one have to worship before the God my mother was trying to make us fear would be the same God of kindness and loving forgiveness grandma always spoke of?

That day I made the decision to hide within myself. I would do what I could to survive this and be, secretly, a different person inside. I would hide who I truly was, and let no one inside my thoughts.

I felt like I had just experienced the ultimate betrayal, and my mother was throwing me to the wolves in the church. I begged her to not make me stay there, or her to stay with me hoping she would protect me. That didn't happen. Too young to understand then, but with a clearer perspective, to me this is what I was feeling but was not mature enough to portray it in words.

You walked away,

You didn't care.

That it was me,

You left standing there.

I reached out to you,

You looked away,

I said good-bye,

Yet begged you stay.

My heart now aches,

Broken in two.

Why pray tell,

I wouldn't do this to you.

Leave you alone,

To feel the pain,

Of emptiness,

And bitter distain.

For my will did cave,

Now I have no more.

You've taken It from me,

My heart a closed door.

I have built my wall,

A fortress none dare get in.

Filled with anger and pain,

That's bottled within.

If you should return,

When saving my soul done.

To tear down these walls,

The Battle's just begun.

-2-

The girl I had met earlier came back into the room and introduced herself to me. Her name was Beth, she then proceeded to recite her 'testimonial' as to how she was a lost sinner trapped in a life filled with Satan and wild ways until God sent her here to meet Brother Mack and she was 'saved' from a life destined for destruction. I silently sat there pretending to listen, while at the same time, I was wondering how long it had taken them to brainwash her into a robotic state of submission. Would that happen to me? Would I eventually cave in and be as submissive and have a 'testimony' of my own? Oh brother, I had better prepare myself for what was to come. But that was not going to be an easy task I would soon learn, I was after all still a child.

Beth told me I could eat soon and then I would be taken to a temporary place to sleep a few hours because I had been on a long road trip and it was getting late. She told me I would need a good rest before I start my new life among the *Followers of Christ*. She stepped out of the room again and I took that moment to glance out the window behind me, and noticed that the sun had started to set and many hours had already passed, perhaps the rest of the days I was to spend here could pass just as quickly. She returned with a sandwich on a plate and a glass of milk. I was famished so I sank my teeth into the sandwich. It was peanut butter, my favorite! About two bites in the sandwich I realized I must have been too hungry to notice on the first bites that there was nothing but peanut butter in trace amounts between those two slices of slightly stale bread, and nothing more.

My mouth began to feel pasty and dry, so I took the glass of milk, which was cold in my hand and went for a healthy swallow. It was cold alright, but it sure didn't taste like regular milk! Aghast and about to vomit, I set the glass on the table. Beth look at me disapprovingly and said, "it's goats milk, and I should be thankful for everything set in front of me as nourishment, because the only nourishment one needs is the nourishing of our sinful souls". When I had finished choking down the rest of the sandwich and the glass of milk, too hungry to care it tasted so bad. Beth then took me down the hall to a tiny musty smelling room that reeked of urine and mold and had no windows. There was a cot sized bed against a wall, with a pillow and a blanket folded at the top of it. There was a doorway on the west wall, and I peered into it and saw it was a bathroom with only a toilet and no sink. She gave me a slight shove towards the bed and told me to sleep. Numbly I stood there and wondered how one could rest in that horrid smell with no window to open and circulate the air in such humidity and stench. I knew this would be a long night. I heard the door slam behind me and the sound of the deadbolt tumbler engage, as if I were a prisoner being locked into a cell. At that moment I really was just too tired to care and curled up onto the bed and threw the blanket over myself, and tried to get some sleep.

Laying, staring at the ceiling with its chipped paint and yellowed hue from lack of cleaning often, I found my mind was full of spinning thoughts and emotions and I couldn't sleep. I kept trying to picture my life at home, the memories I cherished as a very young child and how things had changed when my mother became involved with the Church, and started forcing us to conform to her new fundamentalist beliefs. So much seemed to always be changing in my life and how was I to survive when I never knew what was next?

I recalled my early childhood in comparison to the past few years. Childhood, the most precious and formidable years that mold a being into the productive adult one will become in time, in most circumstances is filled heartily with laughter, joy and minimal hardships. I recall many moments of pleasure and joy in the presence of my grandparents who embraced my creativity and fueled my personality. Outside of my grandparents support, and a few memorable moments of family vacations, the memories that were pleasing get lost in the shuffle of a twisted religious based theory of upbringing my mother had decided to convert us to. I wondered why things had to change so much and why I had chosen to rebel so badly that I wound up here, alone in a dark room, trying not to think of the smell of urine that permeated the darkened room, lit only by a built in night light on the corner of the ceiling, which later I would discover contained a camera for monitoring people.

God is not a bad thing as faith is a foundation of our mere existence. We rely on faith as a mechanism of our hopes for future events. But when religion reaches the point of extremism it becomes the motivator for simple deprivation of one's basic need for self growth and individuality, then it can become the cornerstone to the destruction of free will. I was the type of kid that was full to the gills with free will. This was not a good way to be in these circumstances. My mother was changing into something that scared me and the rules were getting unbearable to my free spirited nature.

We were no longer to partake of any activities outside of a church setting for fear of being victims of Satan's ways. I began to think, either many people in the world were really evil, and I might die if exposed to them or my mother and her fellow believers were totally missing a few screws. But how dare I have any negative thoughts about my mother, as even thinking any negative thought would surely land me in hell. I rebelled. I guess with hindsight now, rebellion should not have been an option I chose.

With every restriction that presented itself, I fought harder to go against it. I was finding myself quite often at the wrong end of a wooden paddle. I wonder if it brought her as much joy as it brought me pain to feel my mother paddle me hard enough I could not sit or defecate for a full day, due to the extreme pain. But none dare breathe a word, as in doing so would result in just more corporal punishment or deprivation of basic necessities as nourishment.

Attempting to flee was not an option, as failed attempts led to further repercussions. My thought was to be so defiant that I would be forced out, or possibly sent to my fathers. That theory did not work, and seeking out my father was difficult due to the lack of contact that my mother saw to. She packed us up and fled to numerous states and church affiliations to keep us from him and his sinful life.

Time passed and I continued to rebel even more. Forced into working to give money to my mother to cover household expenses as she worked and pursued her career was mandatory. Sacrifices had to be made, to put us in private schooling to separate us from the outside world and all its temptations, even if it meant wearing throw away clothes decades old in style, being laughed at and ridiculed by neighbors, and going hungry. Our only reprise was the many trips to my grandmother's. Although very strict in her religious beliefs, my grandmother was naive my mother's extreme methods of keeping us conformed.

Grandma had a gentle but firm kindness that was always comforting. She would so frequently tell us how special we were and do things with us and tell us not to let our mother know some of the "extras" she allowed. It was not until right before my grandmother's death that she acknowledged and told me she wished she could have done more to protect us from our situation, but she too feared the wrath of my mother. Grandmother was raised in an era that you just accept and forgive. She taught us to endure, explaining that you just do not argue with my mother, because she feels she is never wrong.

We must just believe God will watch over us, and that we are not weak when we do not feel the extreme devotion to God that allows some to be consumed to the point of cult like behaviors and thinking. We are after all humans existing in a world created by a forgiving and understanding God who knows we are not perfect. I at that moment hoped that the loving God grandma spoke of would rescue me one day. I knew that this was my future and I will have to just accept it for now. I was trapped among religious extremists, with no escape, well not one I could see yet. I then drifted off to sleep.

-3-

With the blaring of a loud singing pounding in my ears, I was startled and shaken so badly that I rolled off the bed and fell to the floor wondering to myself what the hell was that? I looked up to where the sounds were coming from and when I was able to gain my composure, I realized it was blaring from a speaker on the ceiling, and it must be their sick and twisted way of waking people up in this hell hole. Good thing I was deprived of liquids the majority of the day before, otherwise I am sure it would have startled the pee right out of me, and I would not care to discover the punishment for wetting myself. I folded up the blanket and placed it on the pillow where I had found it, and sat there awaiting the meeting of the first *prison warden* that would come through the door to assault me, and force me to start my day.

I began to straighten my long tussled hair that was in need of proper brushing, adjusted the dress I had been forced to sleep in since it had twisted around my body. Although by now I am sure I smelled a bit ripe from sweat and no clean clothes yet to put on, but still I wanted to feel presentable for my impending doom. Just as I had finished pressing down the skirted portion of my dress I heard a key enter the lock at the door and I was starting into the face once again of that evil Sister Ruth. She was standing there with a face I had not seen before. It was a girl I estimated was about a year or two older than me, and later learned she was 14. Sister Ruth introduced me to her and said she would be my *sister helper*, and teach me the rules, as everyone who was new had an older sister helper to guide them until their permanent buddy was assigned. Her name was Rachel, and she was a little too cheery that early in the morning! All I wanted to do was wash my face and brush my teeth and feel slightly human. She had something else in mind.

We left the room and headed to a group of girls standing outside in even rows so perfectly formed. It reminds me now of prison related movies where inmates were lined up in the courtyard and given messages by a warden. Rachel motioned for me to take my place in the front row next to her and explained that we must start every morning with an opening prayer with our leader, Brother Mack, and then she would show me around and explain the rules of the dormitory, where I would be living. The whole time being reminded I must look down until he arrives to say the morning prayers. I looked down but my eyes were straining to look around and see just how many other girls there were around me. I was reciprocated with nasty glares and gestures to put my eyes where they belong, downward and starting at the ankles of the person I was to be following. There was a sudden wave of hushes and it was if the president had entered the view of everyone around. Dead silence, all but the sounds of nature in the air. A man cleared his throat and I was too scared to look up. Rachel nudged me and said, "look at God's chosen prophet", proudly.

I glanced up to see to a couple that I swore were right out of a horror movie that was twisted. They stood there looking like the Norman Rockwell maw and paw farmers, yet the pitch fork was replaced with a large print King James Version Bible, which the man waived around as he informed us they would preach, paddle and pray the devil out of the camp today, looking directly at me, or so I thought. Of course I would have thought to myself, "OH SHIT", but even in my own altered sense of thought I was afraid to curse even to myself, for fear of God striking me dead. Then he demanded we kneel in the dirt and pray with him, we all started to kneel like submissive slaves awaiting a beating with a whip if we did not, and the long praying commenced. I began to think perhaps that prayer was meant to be more like a stage performance for an audience, than an actual conversation with God. I was busy wishing for breakfast, and wondering what torture some supposed edibles would be tossed before me soon to stop the grumbling in my stomach. He finally finished, and we were all ushered towards the dining hall to eat.

Rows and rows of tables with benches on both sides, made of wood and well worn from usage lined the floors extending almost wall to wall. A cafeteria style set of counters were at the far end, patrolled by women and girls in hairnets and aprons. To the right were two windows into what appeared to be a dish washing area and below it were several cans. A few labeled trash and the others labeled slop written crudely with marker. We all lined up against the wall, everyone had their hands to their sides, facing forward, waiting to get their trays and shuffle down the row of serving counters to collect the morning meal. Rachel whispered to me, "take what they give me and say thank you when they put it on my plate, whether I want or like it or not". She said, "I was to eat as much as I can and not be wasteful, but I must eat at least 75% of what is given". That rule did not seem to bother me all too much, since that was my mother's rule at home. My mother would cook liver, and no matter how much it made me gag we were forced to eat it, just as anything else she cooked that was repulsive or non-palatable, due to lack of seasonings or adequate proportioned ingredients to be considered edible. Breakfast was starting to smell wonderful as I got closer to it. There was bacon, sausage, eggs gravy and toast. At the far end of the serving line there was milk and what looked like plain orange water, being disguised as juice. Recalling how bad the milk was the night before, I opted for the fake juice.

We sat at a table, and began to eat. The food was not bad. The orange beverage was a weakened and over diluted version of Tang®, and tolerable. I thought I could learn to enjoy this, it by far was much more than I was ever privy to in my mother's home when it came to flavor and portions, yet later would discover how tiring that could be when it is the same thing that you will eat every breakfast of every day, except Sundays, which we were treated to two fluffy pancakes. Over time, anything consumed over and over no matter how much you liked it at one time, it will start to become something you despise. When I was done eating, Rachel told me we had to take our trays over and scrape them and place them in the window so the kitchen help could wash them and return to our seats and sit quietly with our hands placed under our butts, so we would not use our hands to gesture or communicate and we were to glance down at the table until we were dismissed to leave the dining hall. We cleared our trays and returned to our seats, and waited.

I began to wonder how these girls could endure always looking down so much, after only about fifteen minutes of that and my neck was beginning to ache. I dared not complain, I did vividly remember the harsh slap across my face the day before when I opened my mouth and said anything. They announced we were dismissed and I watched the girls all line up and file out the doors and head up the road towards another building, I started to head in the same direction, but Rachel said we were heading over to another area so she could show me the dormitory and go over the basic rules of the 'dorm life'. She pointed to a large square building with no windows and several double steel doors, all but one was chained and padlocked shut. I felt a bit uneasy at that moment, and a sense of fear welled up inside me. The sign above the one set of doors unlocked and left propped open, read, G-1. Rachel grasped my arm and pulled hard and told me to hurry, the boys were due to come in from the fields to eat and we must not be seen walking the path at the same time, unless escorted by staff. So we rushed over to the dormitory, making sure not to glance back, as if turning back we would be blinded by God for looking upon the boys. I even sensed the fear in Rachel, as we sped up the road as fast as we could, I still with no shoes, cringing from stepping on pebbles and small objects in the dirt and clay.

We went into the doorway and she removed her shoes and put them in a box along a wall full of small boxes hung from a wall with numbers on them. She explained that every box had a number that matched a bunk inside the sleeping area. My box would be number 45, which was next to hers, since she was in bunk 44 and I would sleep above her for now. She opened another door at the end of the hall, and said this was our sleeping area.

I followed her in. I had never quite seen anything like this before in my life. I figured when she meant bunks, it would be regular bunk beds in rows, this was much worse. They were like double rows of boxes stacked 3 high with only one side to get in and out. She walked over to one set in the far corner at the end of a row. I counted the sets as we passed them, and there were 8. The room seemed so small because there were several rows all cramped together with no windows and bad lighting. The smell was as if I had just stuffed my head into a laundry hamper of sweaty sport clothes and socks. I was rapidly becoming nauseated. It didn't seem to bother Rachel. I guess you get used to it over time. I sure hope so, or I would be losing my guts often.

Now as I close my eyes and think back, it reminds me so much of a concentration camp seen in old movies of Nazi Germany, and the thought sends chills down my spine.

She motioned to my bunk and told me I would sleep on the top one, she was in the middle, and the bottom was for someone younger that had been there a while and the climb to the top bunk was too hard for them. I asked, "How do I get up there"? She replied, "Stand on the ones below and climb up." That really was not too hard to do, since they were close enough together in height, and not like standard bunk beds, you could not sit up when on any of the beds below. She told me I could climb up to my bunk and she would hand me some bedding and I could make my bed while she gathered the dorm rules to go over with me and then later show me around more. I climbed up and started to wrestle the sheet onto the piece of yellow, smelly foam rectangle that was to be considered a mattress since it was covered in a thick plastic encasement with tape over a few places I assumed must have been tears or holes covered up to extend its use, and it was the only thing there besides a flat pillow that smelled much worse. I was beginning to wonder if these people were so set on cleansing the soul from sin did they forget to wash their bodies. Or perhaps does it get so hot in that dorm with no windows that sweat is the only thing that permeates around here? I had a wool blanket she handed me I neatly attempted to tuck in around the edges of the boxed frame and climbed down. She told me. "We must make our beds every morning right after we get out of them except on the first of every month, when we were to pull our sheets off the bed and put them with our blankets into the pillow case that was way too large for our pillows and carry them to the laundry".

Now it was time for the 'dorm rules' and the basic schedule. It was lengthy but basically boiled down to simple degradation.

- No talking unless spoken to, studying scriptures with your assigned buddy, or talking to an elder.

- 1 washcloth and towel is assigned per week, if you lose them, you do not get another until the next Saturday.

- Wake up is at 5 am unless you're on a work crew specified to be awake at 4:30 am. You have 15 minutes to ready yourself and dress for morning schedules. No showering in the morning.

- No braiding of your hair, it must be in a pony tail or cut.
- Follow the bathroom rules. (Those I would learn later were awful in themselves).

- We have breakfast after am chores, go to school until lunch, then work until afternoon chapel, then more work, supper, then showers, and prayers and scripture memorization, then one last chapel service over the speakers before bed at 8 pm.

Rachel explained there are many other rules I will learn as I go and that most of them wasted too much paper to write out.

I told her I had to use the restroom and she said she would show me where it is and then after I read those posted rules, she would show me where my clothes were and where I would keep my toothbrush and soap. As we walked to the bathroom she explained to me that for the first few days I will do chores with her until I was assigned my other buddy who I would work and spend every waking moment with and that is rotated as needed sometimes monthly as were chores. But today I would stay with her learning more about the place and getting my things put away before evening chores and supper. Tomorrow we would follow the schedule and in a day or so if I could be trusted to comply, I would be with my buddy.

The bathroom had a large poster at each end thumb-tacked to a blue wall. The rules are easy to remember, because I had several times a day to sit upon one of the porcelain thrones and read them, trying to ignore the other girls around me, as there were no walls between any of the long row of commodes lined across one wall with the equivalent amount of sinks in a row along the wall directly across from them all stained with rust from well water. At the far end was what looked like a cube lined with tiles and several shower heads as the place we were to shower. Next to that was a stretch of hooks along a wall, and above them was a sign reading, "Thou shalt not steal".

I felt odd having to sit there and try to relieve myself with someone watching me. It was different growing up and using the bathroom when my sister was around but these were total strangers. But I had to go pretty bad and was not going to squabble about an audience. I did notice there were only toilet paper rolls along the wall on hooks, and as I was reading the rules while commencing to my business, I understood why it was on a wall. Two squares for regular use and 4 squares with approve permission. Girls needing personal products must have verification first. Showers were 5 minutes. A short list but it definitely required explaining.

I understood what the squares meant, but who counted them? Rachel explained, "The *dorm leaders* (girls brainwashed and put in charge to enforce the rules) always handed them to each other so as not to cheat and take more". Then I asked, "What was meant by verification for needs"? Boy was I horrified at the response I got! She explained that as a group we used the restroom in an orderly fashion. We must line up and wait our turn. When it was our turn we were given our ration of 2 squares of toilet tissue. If we were to dare request more, we had to announce the purpose of the need for more in front of everyone in the dorm bathroom line.

I was content to know, being that I had not yet reached my menstrual cycle, I would not be further humiliated by the need to request the issuance of hygiene products, and be forced to drop my undergarments for inspection to verify the presence of menstrual blood on my body to a minimum of two 'big sisters' and staff. They must confirm that it was a valid request. I prayed hard every day to myself that as my breasts began to develop, that I wouldn't be cursed to the humiliation of having my period too!

From the moment those rules were brought to my attention, I could feel my insides boiling with rage. I felt a confused anger and hate for this "God" my grandmother had taught me to love, and an even deeper hatred for my mother who placed me there. It was not the loving God I knew from my childhood attending Sunday school who performed so many miracles written in the scriptures, and great actions meant to bring joy and love to the world. Where the hell was I, because this certainly wasn't planet earth?

I felt slightly dizzy from all the rules swimming in my head and I couldn't understand how this could actually be a way to live, a life of forced conformity to communal living for the sake of Christianity and salvation of my wayward soul. Would I survive this? I began to wonder if there truly were two Gods and how would the right one find and rescue me. I felt lost, scared, and alone. How could my mother have sent me there, and just left me?

We went back out to the dorm sleeping area and across the room to another doorway, and Rachel said this was where we were to put our things. It was like a closet almost 40 feet long and about 6 feet wide. There were cords from lights dangling about every 4 feet from the ceiling, and numbers dangling on cards attached to the bottoms of each cord. We were by the fourth light since we were in bunks numbered between 40 and 50. To the right of the huge closet was a long pole that spanned the full length of the wall, with several supports all labeled just like the lights, in order as they progressed. On the pole I noticed red striped every foot or so and a white stripe separating sets of sections of the red stripes. Every hanger that was placed on the pole was neatly between all the lines, and none touching each other. I thought to myself, oh crap! I barely hung anything up let alone neatly on a hanger. This would take getting used to. She took me down to a section and I recognized a few of my dresses hanging in a section with a wooden cubicle below it and the number 45 painted on it in a bright ugly green color. That was to be where I put my underwear, socks and personal belongings. Above the hanging clothes was a spot for about 3 pairs of shoes and I saw my sneakers sitting there and asked if I could please put them on, my feet were sore from walking barefoot all morning. I was allowed to, and it felt so much better not to be walking on the floors that felt gritty and gross on my toes. I asked why the spaces were so little, and Rachel said, "We do laundry every week, so a person only needs clothing for a week". "Personal possessions were forbidden in the dormitory unless we had earned the privilege to move to the *converted souls dorm* where true believers found worthy eventually got to live. I knew right then, that would be a dorm I would never see, I was not going to give in to this nonsense. I was going to rebel until I was kicked out, or so I thought. It was close to lunch so we headed back over to the dining hall and then off to chores and the second half of my first day. I was rapidly becoming quite irritated with everything but decided I had better just keep that thought to myself.

-4-

Lunch was something I could either adapt to or leave behind. A sandwich with some kind of spreadable chicken salad with enough to perhaps cover a cracker or two, but not enough to be considered a true sandwich, a pear that was mushy, over ripe and bruised as if someone had used it for a game of catch, and a glass of some undefined fruit beverage, or so I assumed since it was colored red and near flavorless. It was food anyway, so I ate it. Rachel and I then headed to do assigned afternoon chores. She said, "Today we were to feed the hens and collect eggs and wash them, then clean out the hen house and head to the troughs". So I thought this probably was not going to be too bad, and thousands of farmers have done this daily for centuries, I could handle it.

Oh Hell! I now know where all the demons they supposedly cast out of people went! They went to the pen connected to the hen house. Within seconds of getting thru the gated entry, here they came, not only pecking on the ground at the food we scattered all over, but all over us, pecking our legs and chasing us as we ran all around to get away from them. I can imagine in dresses with pecked up legs and screaming we were quite a sight to anyone passing by. We then went into the hen house and it went downhill from there. Not only did the satanically possessed chickens peck my legs, but my arms and ears too as we ran around grabbing eggs from inside the nesting boxes making the chickens even madder and peck harder. Then all of a sudden here it came, Satan Rooster himself, as Rachel was explaining to me why he was so named that, I discovered why.

He chased after me and pinned me into a corner and proceeded to peck the daylights out of my ankles until I kicked him away and ran out of there as fast as I could with him taking chase and pecking at me all the way. Rachel came out behind me just laughing as hard as she could, then she told me the best way to handle the rooster is to squawk at him loudly and walk backwards and it will intimidate him, and when I walk backwards bob up and down like he does. I thought to myself, you have got to be kidding? So not only do I get to be treated like a prisoner all day, every day, but now I have to wave my arms around , scream at animals and act like a resident in a psychiatric facility.

We spent about two hours cleaning out the pen and I felt like I had worked for three days, it was so hot and humid I could have taken a shower in my own sweat, and felt ill from the smell. I was rapidly becoming angry with my mother for sending me here.

"It was time to head to our next chore, the troughs, before supper followed by quiet time and then group prayer meeting and bed", Rachel said. I was ready to go to bed now. I was already tired from everything we did so far, and never recovered from the lack of sleep I experienced on the two day road trip to get here. So off to the troughs we went, I was thinking to myself this won't be too bad, I survived the chickens from hell. How wrong I was once again! Anyone that has driven down a country road in the heat of the summer, and passed a pig farm will relate to the horrid stench it can create. The only difference is, when you drive past it, eventually the smell rapidly fades. When you have to work in it for over an hour it will make your insides turn.

Rachel and I went to the dining hall for supper, and I was still so sick to my stomach from the smell of the pigs, and having to wade through pig crap that I spent my evening meal time with my head buried in a trash can throwing up. By the time my stomach settled, I was being pulled by my arm to go to the evening prayer meeting, and being told by Sister Ruth, "either suck it up or go to the isolation hole". As shitty as this place was, and as bad as I already felt, I sure did not want to find out what the *isolation hole* was, at least not today.

We had to quickly wash our hands and faces, grab our Bibles and head to the evening prayer meeting. “It is 20 licks and a week of double chores if we are late, Rachel said, with sense of fear in her voice. So we ran as fast as we could to the meeting hall chapel, and got into the last row right before they shut the doors to start. I was wondering what ‘licks’ were but really was not in any rush to find out.

I really did not believe anyone here believes in good hygiene and air conditioning, because there we sat all packed in one huge room on metal folding chairs elbow to elbow and barely any room to move, with a few fans blowing, and no windows. The smell of that many sweaty people made me feel like I had hopped into a basket of sweaty athletic clothing that had not been washed in a week but instead had been baked in the sun.

I found myself fighting to keep from gagging, and was relieved when they said everyone must spend the first twenty minutes kneeling on the concrete with our hand on the chairs and heads bowed in prayer. I saw it as the perfect opportunity to bury my head in my hands, pinch my nose closed to try and block the smell and catnap. It seemed to have worked, since I didn't fall victim to any retribution, and the *devotional* part of the meeting was to commence. Brother Mack got up and yelled, commanding us, "Rise to your feet and look at each other, you unworthy sinners". Everyone jumped to their feet, as if GOD had spoken, and looked around then back at him. "You are all as filthy, as the swine in the pens, and must daily repent", he spoke firmly, as he slammed his large print Bible onto the pulpit, scaring half the girls in the room, as they gasped and my heart nearly skipped a beat in fear.

We spent about another hour listening to Brother Mack rant about the worthless pieces of crap we were as humans before he finally decided it was time for an alter call, and those who felt they had to confess their wrong doings could come up front and fall onto the floor of the stairs below the platform and pulpit and beg and cry for Brother Mack to ask God to save us from our sinful selves. They played some piano music as Brother Mack was saying over and over, "Come kneel and repent"! Girls began to fill the aisles heading down front crying and begging, and I was thinking to myself, there really are way too many freaks and too few circuses. That lasted about ten minutes and we were dismissed to go to the dormitory and get our showers and then sleep. I was ecstatic! Finally a shower and a bed, knowing that my bed was a crap piece of foam, I was so tired, I didn't care.

Off to a shower in groups of six and use the five minutes of ice cold water the best we could, before the water was cut off, and drying ourselves, we headed to our bunks. I laid there with my head on my pillow and thought to myself, ah... I had survived day one.

-5-

In the early hours of the morning, the sun had not even risen and I was shaken awake by Rachel, who said that she was "chosen to do some of God's work singing in the group choir and traveling for a week with Brother Mack", and she wanted to share the news before everyone else was awake and she would already be gone. There was just enough time to hurry and pack since she would be leaving in a few minutes and wanted to let me know that I would be with a different *sister helper* when everyone got up and later have a new assigned *buddy*. She told me to "take care and that I would see her upon her return", and advised me to follow the rules and "let go of Satan and I would one day find his will for me". I said "okay", and didn't dare speak what I was thinking. Surely I was NOT the one hanging onto something that needed to be let go of. These people needed to let go of the pedestal they had that wacko Brother Mack on.

Trumpets sounded in the background, as the loud speaker crackled out the daily message in ear damaging decibels, "RISE AND MAKE HASTE, THE SERVANTS OF THE LORD MUST WORK AND SHOW THEMSELVES WORTHY FOR THE MASTER"! I clasped my hands to my pained ears, as I stumbled to the floor, half asleep, mumbling under my breath, "these people are insane"! The speakers were no further than 4 feet above where I slept, mounted on a little bracket that was missing some necessary hardware and shook when it blared. I was happy that the bracket was still sturdy enough to keep it from falling and knocking me out. I rubbed the sleep from my weary eyes as I straightened my covers before heading to the 5 minutes allotted dress and freshen up time. I would then get the pleasure of standing along the wall for inspection by staff and ushered out with my new assigned tormentor to start the ritualistic grind I would now be calling my daily routine.

I washed my face, dressed and stood along the wall, waiting. Sister Ruth was standing there with paddle in hand and bellowed out in her ear piercing tone, "Everyone kneel for the daily hem check". We were told to place our hands atop of our head and stand on our knees, and the hem of our skirts must touch the floor. If the hems were above the floor, girls were pulled from the line and reprimanded harshly for allowing the thigh to show. As Sister Ruth put it, "showing of the thigh is exposing man to temptation by revealing flesh to be only seen as God saw fit". One of many rules I became accustomed to when it came to clothing. We were not allowed to wear any short sleeves unless the sleeves were no more than 4 inches above the elbows. All dresses must have slips under them. NO shorts, no pants, no emblems or logos. No tee shirts. Are they sure this isn't a convent? All blouses must be buttoned to the top, if no buttons then dresses or shirts must come open at the neckline no lower than 2 fingers below the top of the breastplate bone. All clothing must be loose enough that the figure cannot be defined, and no undergarment lines visible while standing or bending. Dressed like that I could easily see why no guy would ever want to look at us, we looked like we were from centuries past. Top it off, in the hot Louisiana heat working on a farm, the attire was a prison for heat beyond the imagination. I felt like I was in a personal sauna almost daily, and lusted for winter.

Once the hem check was completed Sister Ruth called me to the side and introduced me to the other girl I would be paired up with for the rest of the week. Her name was Amy and she seemed way too happy that early in the morning as she introduced herself to me, “HI, I’m Amy, and I am a follower of Christ”. I said, “Hi, that’s nice, when do we eat breakfast?” She gave me a disapproving look and said, “We eat shortly, and God is more important than food and you should always remember that”.

Our assignments were handed to us and we proceeded out to the front gravel-covered meeting place outdoors where Brother Mack was going to give his morning spew about how we were all worthless sinners and unworthy to walk the earth God created, and then a long prayer before we could have our morning meal.

Off to breakfast, silently we sat and ate, the same as the day before, and every day to come, eggs with no salt or pepper, biscuits you could play baseball with and they wouldn't crumble, gravy and sausage. Now that may sound excellent, but as I said before, we ate this every morning, six days a week, and what I would have given to have a piece of toast with peanut butter on it, or even my mother's flavorless oatmeal on occasion would have been a welcome change. We collected our trays and utensils and headed out to start our daily chores. Amy said the rest of the week we were not going to school and that we would be doing chores because the teachers had special meetings they had to attend for a few weeks to keep the government from closing the homes down. We were going to spend our days doing chores until school resumed the next month. That was fine with me, after one day of school I had my fill anyway.

Instead of heading to the hen house, we were headed towards a few rundown looking barns off in the distance. As we drew closer, the smell was almost overwhelming. I had never smelled anything so horrid in my life! There it was directly in front of me, a whole pen full of squealing pigs, wallowing in their own filth and excrement mixed with mud and old hay. I leaned over the fence and everything I had for breakfast came right back up so fast that it was like someone had turned a faucet on. "Someone please shoot me", I thought as my stomach wretched in pain from the gagging and dry heaves that were to follow. Amy reassured me that I would get used to the smell. She handed me a jar of vapor rub that had a label worn off and initials etched on it, and told me to put some under my nose before I worked, and told me not to tell anyone she had found it when helping in the *Followers of Christ* dorm for the girls that had been there for a while and were allowed to have special things we were not allowed to have.

I asked Amy how girls earned getting to move to that dorm and what different things did they get to have. She said, "They get to have items from in town and notebooks and pens and paper, and coloring books and mirrors. They also get to do their chores and walk around with their friends they make and do not have a buddy all the time and have bathrooms with stalls". She said that the weeks upcoming she would get to move there because she had given her testimony of her salvation from sin and had followed the rules. I thought to myself, "I have to get to that dorm, no matter what it takes. I decided at that moment I was going to have to learn to play along and get to that place, and then I could be able to have a notebook and write and draw, which was something I really loved to do. That dorm even had windows! I must get there and soon!

Inside the stalls with the pigs, shoveling pig poop into wheel barrels, I found myself almost knee deep in crap. We had to scoop it up and then roll the wheel barrels down the side of a hill, to the fire pits which were spots where the waste was burned along with trash and other things. It smelled real bad there too, and by the time lunch had approached, food was the furthest thing from my mind. We headed to get to the dining hall, making sure to hose off our shoes outside the building with a garden hose, before going in. Sister Ruth met us at the door, and looked at everyone's feet as they entered. She got to me and huffed, then grabbed me by the arm and yanked me back out the door, yelling at me the whole time. "You are filthy as the pigs, and shall be punished for uncleanliness", she said. I said, "But I was working with the pigs and had no boots, I tried to clean it off, but I was knee deep in poop and mud". She harshly grabbed my shoulder and whipped me around over the fence and proceeded to whip me with the paddle that hung from a rope tied to her belt, around her waist that was about as round as a trash barrel.

I cried and begged her to stop and promised I would never have dirty shoes again. She then stopped and told me, "You will not be allowed to wear shoes while working for the rest of the month". I was hoping she was joking, but I could not be so lucky. She took my shoes from me and told me they would be inside the door on the shelf where the rest of the slobs put their shoes until they were done working. I went into the dining hall and ate lunch, dreading the afternoon, but remembering in my mind what Amy had said about the other dorm, and knew I will have to start following the rules if I wanted to get to go there and have notebooks and a pencil to write. This was going to be a task in itself, but I was on a mission, and as stubborn as I am, I knew I could do it, and I was determined to do so.

-6-

Two weeks had passed and I was starting to get adjusted to life on the compound. Early wakeups by blaring speakers, communal bathrooms and showers, crappy food and manual labor until blisters rose on our hands, was becoming commonplace. I managed to not get into any trouble and knew that just one more week and I shall have my shoes back, and no more wallowing in the pig pen barefoot. No more running from chickens and having them peck the daylights out of my toes until they bled. Amy and I were getting along and I started paying close attention to how she acted and behaved around staff, and imitated everything she did in hopes to one day get into the other dorm that she would be going to in a few days. I remembered to make sure to not make any comments unless asked, I always said, “Yes Ma’am” and “sir”, and minded the rules and even started memorizing the retarded songs that they made us learn and sing.

The day had arrived and Amy was whisked away to the other dorm, and I was left with an empty feeling again. Even though part of me thought she was a bit nutty, she was kind to me and helped me stay focused when I started to stray towards any behavior that would result in serious punishment. Who would I be stuck with next? I cannot recall her name, so I will just name her Jane, and she was evil, clear to the bone EVIL! Being that she was a leader sister and I was still considered wayward, she was superior to me and I had to not only listen to staff but also tolerate her bossiness. I was considered wayward because I had not thrown myself upon an altar during religious services and confessed my evil ways and asked for forgiveness from Brother Mack and God. That also meant I was doomed to listen to her daily reminding me I was going to burn in Hell for not doing so. Just when I was starting to get the hang of things, she comes along and totally screwed up my plans to fake my way through this. She was the type of person you just couldn't help but defy.

After two days of her nagging and pestering me over every little thing, I had my fill. We were in the hen house collecting eggs and she was telling me I should learn to pray better and sing praises and quote scriptures from the Bible as I worked instead of staying silent. Then she pushed me down to the floor of the hen house and shoved my face into chicken poop. Which was not hard for her to do considering she towered my by at least a foot and was a good forty pounds thicker than me. She proceeded to walk to the other side of the hen house and yelled at me, "collect those eggs, and be fast about it". I wiped my face on my skirt and turned to collect eggs. I was so overwhelmed with anger that I could not control what was about to happen next. With reddened face and full of rage, I was overcome with so much disdain for Jane, that before I could stop, I found myself reaching into nesting boxes, grabbing eggs as fast as I could and throwing them at

Jane's head like a well oiled military machine one after the other, hitting my target at the dead center of her forehead. She screamed so loud when she fled the hen house, that Sister Ruth and two other staff cronies came running at full speed towards me in a manner that scared the shit out of me and I knew I was doomed. But I didn't care; I would take any punishment they were to dish out if it meant I would have five minutes away from her. Or so I thought.

The two male cronies that came in tow behind Sister Ruth grabbed me by each arm and started hauling me up the gravel and dirt road towards Brother Mack's office. They were dragging me by my arms in such a fast manner that it hurt my shoulders. Sister Ruth trailed behind rebuking me, as my feet drug the ground and skin on the tops of them were shedding skin until they stung in pain. They stopped and Sister Ruth came from behind me and slapped me then opened Brother Mack's door and they pulled me in and let go of me. I fell to the floor grabbing my feet, crying. Blood was coming from the torn away skin and the more I cried the more I was yelled at. Sister Ruth went over to a cabinet and pulled out a bottle of alcohol and said, “Stop crying, shut up, and let me clean your feet and maybe some of the devil in you will leave with the filth”. I gasped as the cold alcohol touched the open sores, and bit my tongue so hard that I felt like part of it was going to fall right out of my mouth from being bitten in half. Brother Mack then entered his office, and I would soon learn the fate of my actions.

I was sentenced to punishment row, which meant I was not allowed to eat meals with any of the other girls. I was to spend two days eating with the other girls who were facing the same fate for actions that were not considered acceptable conduct on the compound. I would eat bread and water for lunch and dinner, and was to spend the rest of my time on my knees in prayer or reading the Bible in a room we had secretly named *Hell Hall*. I was to always face the wall with my hands over my head when waiting in any line. We were to sleep in there on the floor each night, and were not allowed to shower, wash or brush our teeth for the duration. Of course this was quite harsh, but I no longer had to listen to Jane run her mouth or walk through pig shit to work, at least for a few days anyway. By the time my punishment was over, I had felt like there was no other option but to conform, to be who they wanted me to be, whether I liked it or not. I would start playing their game, and I would start that day.

I decided that evening at our chapel service, I would begin my 'change', and repent. But how does one cry when they truly are not repentant? One can wail and seem remorseful, but how do I create tears, when inside I was full of so much hate? Then it hit me. I could ask for some alcohol on a cotton ball to clean the sores on my feet, and stash one for later and use it to make my eyes hurt and tears flow. I asked to go to see the nurse, and was taken there and she gave me some peroxide on a few pieces of gauze. I was not sure if it would sting and make my eyes water later, but I had to make an effort and try if I were to survive and do this. I waited until she turned to put the peroxide back in the cabinet and stashed one of the peroxide covered gauze squares in the waistband of my skirt, and proceeded to casually clean my wounds with the rest. She smiled at me and put some first aid cream on them, and I left to return to my daily routine. It was drawing close to evening service time, and as we were finishing up our chores, I decided to start smiling and humming songs with the other girls working, Jane by my side, singing, and all the while wanting to just punch her instead. But I was on a mission and I was going to be smarter than them. I was going to fool them all!

We had our evening meal, and then headed to the dorm to wash our faces and use the restroom before it was time to meet at the chapel for the service and the alter call to follow. This would be where I do my grand performance and hope it fools somebody, anybody. I had to if I were to try and survive these nuts. Escaping wasn't an option because that fence was just way too high and the staff said outside of them were alligators in swamps waiting to get us. As a kid, heck who wouldn't believe that after seeing a few skeletal remains of alligators nailed to one of the fences along the animal pens?

The service began and my mind was racing with so many thoughts about my plan that it drowned out anything that was being said during the sermon. Not that I would have listened anyway, but I am sure if our brains could overheat from excessive racing thoughts, mine would have had smoke not only rolling out both my ears but my nose too and my eyes would have cooked like boiled eggs and rolled out onto the floor. Then I heard Brother Mack make the invitational for those repentant soul to come up from and throw themselves to the altar. I had seen so many other girls do it, and now my time had come. It was all planned in my head, and time for a grand performance. I quickly took the peroxide laden gauze pad to my eyes hidden under a Kleenex and rubbed it on them. Ouch did that ever sting and make my eyes water. I made my way to the aisle from the center or the row of chairs I was in and headed down from wailing and wiping tears from my eyes, and instead of crying out that my eyes were on fire from exposure, I begged the people at the altar to ask God to have mercy on me, and I was a sinner in need of God.

I heard Sister Ruth and several others approach me saying, "Praise God, Hallelujah, and amen", all the while thinking to myself, "By golly I think I pulled it off"! I told Sister Ruth that I wanted to follow the right path (I heard enough of the other girls supposedly repent and knew what to say). She hugged me, and I wanted to puke, but said, "Thank you Sister Ruth for guiding me", and hugged her back. That was a major boost to her ego. For the next few days she was extra nice to me and I smiled and acted like I really cared about God and everyone there, when instead I was plotting how to get into the other dorm and possibly with a bit more freedom, plan an escape.

As each day passed I seemed to plunge further into the world of "New Bethany religion", I felt as if pieces of my soul became detached, and I was losing who I was, and who I could become, to the wasting away of my will. Could people really believe that this type of existence would truly warrant them a fancier castle upon the streets of gold in a heaven so beautifully paved by a loving God? This truly could not be the same God grandma spoke about because these people have twisted it into their own ideology to suit their own pleasures for their so-called "Master".

School was back in session and it was becoming very hard to follow the rules and attend classes but I was holding out as best I could. Sister Ruth told me that I was being a loyal servant of God's chosen one Brother Mack and that soon I may be promoted to the other Dorm, and I was ecstatic. My plan was working. Then the day came, and I was to move. YES! I knew this was going to be great. I would get the chance to have a notebook and writing materials, and I would get to work without an annoying buddy, and have personal things from the store and a mirror. No longer would I have to use the restroom and shower in the presence of another. And it had windows. Oh the windows! We could open them on hot evenings and feel a breeze flow. I was excited. This would be much easier than the dorm I was in currently, although it would still be hard because of having to pretend I was someone I was not.

-7-

Still no television, or radio, or newspapers and ungodly items, but I was settling down in the new dorm, and a bit happier for the freedoms my acting had allowed. I was becoming quite the young actress. I was allowed notebooks and paper to take notes of a religious nature, and frequently our books were taken and checked. So I would have to find a means of hiding what I wrote that was unacceptable. At least hide my poetry until I could memorize it well enough and dispose of the evidence. I was adapting and learning to hide who I was inside, and although I had a few more freedoms as a result of this role playing and performance, it came with a price.

I would see Brother Mack and the staff now smiling as I would stroll by singing their songs and praises as I passed, and not the scornful look I had experienced in the past. But when I would return to my dorm and look into the mirror, it was hard, because I did not like what I saw. It was not me, it was not who I was inside. I was beginning to think I was changing too much. So much, that it was if I were staring into the eyes of a stranger. I started to write poetry about how I felt and then put it to memory and hid the small pieces of paper inside my shoes when I would work. When I had chores that required getting my feet wet or dirty I found an old crevice in the back of the clothing closet where the corners didn't meet all the way and would fold papers up and hide them there for safe keeping. One of the poems I wrote was asking God or anyone in heaven if they had forgotten me or would remember me and rescue me one day. Because I truly believed that the God these people knew and the God my grandmother talked about were two different Gods and someone had to be hearing me up there. Inside I felt, if someone didn't rescue me soon I might as well just be dead, and some days I wanted to just die instead of always having to pretend.

As I lay my head down one more night,
Are you listening God, do you feel my fright?
Please release me from this prison so bleak,
One day, I beg you, for freedom I seek.

I know you hear me and I pray that you can,
Please show me some sign, I know that you can.
I cannot bear these confining walls,
I feel so lost, I don't know 'me' at all.

If nothing else, just help me through,
For I cannot make it, if not for you.
I feel if I stay, I shall not last,
My will shall fade, and I shall pass.

I must practice better survival skills to make it through this. So I would adapt by writing my thoughts and feelings and write poetry as often as I could when I was supposed to be writing notes about scriptures I was allegedly studying. Although hard to do, I managed. I had plenty of practice in the world of religion. No Matter how hard I fought to be an individual with my own thoughts and feelings, I felt as if I were trapped only inches from a path of escape, yet no means to seek it. Years later I composed this poem to reflect the emotional turmoil it created, as I battled whether their teachings were to be my destiny or were they there to warp me into a clone of their making. I felt caged in a world I didn't belong to.

I am caged, I roar, but does anyone hear?

My longing is pain, my time is near.

Relief so close...a portal away,

Dare I cross over, or stay another day.

The human hidden within, longs to be free,
Can I escape it, or is it now part of me?
Am I destine for this, how long do I wait,
My desire to pursue...that open gate?

The once master of the key, to unlock my realm,
Reality since drifted away, who is left at the helm?

I claw and then retreat, the urge so strong,
To break free and be where I belong.
If I so choose, what will the result be,
The need to unleash free will is hidden in me.

When desire outweighs, the strength to restrain,
Will it cause confusion, or harbor great pain?

I pace, my gait, becoming a powerful force,

I must soon break free, will there be recourse?

Decisiveness a drawback, yet the decision a clue,

Is this the time to withdraw, or seek something new.

I must choose to go, or choose to stay,

So I wonder this moment, how and which way?

How toxic can it be to one, when they learn to play the game of life proficiently as an early teen? Depends on who is playing the game and with whom. Playing the role of one individual and hiding my true identity was like being two people trapped in one body. I learned to *play* the game, the role of *fundamentalist youth* well before I even had the skills to drive a car. I became an actress so refined and tuned to the desires of the audience for which my grand performance would be viewed. The only toxicity was the blackening of my heart towards my audience.

My role included but was not limited to total dedication and devotion to the *cause*. That cause being indentured servitude to the leader of the compound and his 'God', until the time of one's physical demise, and freedom sought was to be everlasting life in a heavenly setting graced by the luxuries that were based on earthly works. We would serve him by seeing to the needs of the compound and in service to God through total dedication of song and word.

During the week we would work the farm tilling, planting, harvesting and storing food for the seasons. Then attend a school for a few hours to further our education, then back to work on the farmland until sunset, when we would wash and dress for evenings of prayer and worship at the chapel.

I remember many a time we were awakened at 3 to 4 am, made to dress, meet at the chapel and pray for hours for the lost souls in the community outside the compound. Mainly the prayers were at the behest of leaders to pray that God would strike brimstone down upon the souls of the state organizations that wanted to breech the compound and close them down.

I became well versed in the 'prayers' wanted to be heard, the scriptures required quoting and the demeanor expected. To this day I can call to memory approximately over 400 King James Version passages that have been embedded through their demands. Most of which to me have a different meaning than the one they portrayed.

I even learned all the songs they required us to sing. Some are common to most fundamentalist groups today and some written by their own staff which portrays a sense of warped ideology. What I find even more disturbing is an anti-evolution song I was forced to sing, that I have caught myself humming to this day. I am not sure of its author, but remember it being sung before on a Jerry Falwell program also. Grab some antacid you will need it for the lyrics;

I'm no kin to the monkey no no no,
The monkey's no kin to me yeah yeah yeah,
I don't know much about his ancestors,
But mine didn't swing from a tree.

It seems so unbelievable,
And yet they say that it's true,
They're teaching us about it in school now,
That humans were monkeys once too.

Oooo I'm no kin to the monkey no no no,
The monkey's no kin to me yeah yeah yeah,
I don't know much about his ancestors,
But mine didn't swing from a tree.

Although it's so ridiculous,
They're teaching us now that it's true,
The teachers that came from a monkey,
Would be better off in a zoo.

Oooo I'm no kin to the monkey no no no,
The monkey's no kin to me yeah yeah yeah,
I don't know much about his ancestors,
But mine didn't swing from a tree.

It seems so much more believable,
And surely, surely it's true,
That God made Man in His image,
No monkey story will do.

Oooo I'm no kin to the monkey no no no,
The monkey's no kin to me yeah yeah yeah,
I don't know much about his ancestors,
But mine didn't swing from a tree,

This monkey business has to go,
Because it just isn't true,
It's such a disgrace to the monkey,
A disgrace to the human race too.

Oooo I'm no kin to the monkey no no no,
The monkey's no kin to me yeah yeah yeah,
I don't know much about his ancestors,

But mine didn't swing from a tree,

Mine didn't swing from a tree,

Mine didn't swing from a tree.

Imagine the mental instability one would feel they are experiencing, when thirty years later; one would catch themselves humming that subconsciously? I had contemplated on a few occasions a possible commitment to a local facility for lunatics. Then reality sets in and I have to remind myself of the remote possibility, if I do that, they just might keep me and not let me loose! My writing was my only means of survival, my therapy.

I was called to the side one day and told by Sister Ruth that she was proud that I had found *the way of the Lord,* and one day I would be chosen for a special calling to show my dedication to God's chosen leader, Brother Mack. I was not sure what that meant at that time but soon would learn, it was not a rewarding experience.

-8-

A few more weeks had passed and I wasn't quite sure how long I had been there. Time passes and with no calendars allowed one loses track of days and weeks. It was a brisk morning, the sun was not up yet and the usual bellowing over the loud speakers had not occurred, when I was awakened from my sleep and forced out of bed and told by Sister Ruth, I was to be "sanitized of any residual sin and be presented". I was escorted to a small cottage across the pasture, and left to sit inside the doorway of the cottage. Sister Ruth said, "You must sit and wait a few minutes and the assistants will be here to come and prepare you for God's calling, and proclamation of your loyalty to Brother Mack".

I sat there and begin to look around. I saw just a few menial pieces of furniture in the main room I was sitting in and 2 doors. One to the left was opened and was a kitchen like area that was very small and had only the basics and a table with 2 chairs. To the right was a door drawn most of the way closed, so I raised off the chair and stretched my arm out as far as I could without being too distant from the seat and pushed it open a bit to see inside. It was an all- white room with a bed, a very big bed at that, all covered in white linens and white curtains hung from the ceiling surrounding the four corners of it. It looked too clean to be a part of this cottage whose exterior was run down and in shambles. I noticed there was a bathroom off the room that had a bath tub. That was something I never knew even existed on this compound. I hurriedly sat down before someone returned to catch me peeking around. I was not sure what to think.

I was getting restless, I reached to try the door handle and maybe take a peek outside since it had been a while, and I was wondering if they forgot me. The door was locked from the outside. Fear started to fill my body as I sat there awaiting what would happen next. I had heard rumors from the other girls, but had never spoken to anyone that had proclaimed their loyalty and spoke of it. I sat there shaking as panic enthroned my body, I trembled. Truly submission to one of God's servants did not mean what I had heard from my *big sisters?* Or did it? Or was that all rumors? What was going to happen next, should I run for my life and dare get over that barbed wire fence, or were the tales and rumors untrue? I heard footsteps coming, no time to make a move. I was destined by fate to whatever was to befall me next.

Sister Ruth came back in the door of the cottage with 2 ladies. She introduced me to them and then left me alone with them. They were smiling and singing gospel songs and repeatedly telling me that I was blessed to be chosen by Brother Mack personally, and they would ready me for the calling to his service. They led me by the hand to the bathroom and had me sit on a stool and ran a bathtub of hot water for me. Then they started to remove my clothing, but not as harshly as they were removed the day I arrived here at the compound. I was numb and too afraid to fight because I remembered all the hits and bruises I sustained the first time I fought and figured I would receive the same rebuking and punishment if I did.

They left the room. I thought I perhaps would be left alone to wash and soak and enjoy. The water was almost too hot and it felt kind of like I was a lobster stuck in a boiling pot and my skin turned a bright pink, yet it was the first warm water cleansing I had experienced since I had been here, and I was savoring every moment of the warmth. That thought didn't last long as both women returned arms loaded with miscellaneous items in tow. They placed the items on the counter and stool and proceeded to head towards me with a huge brush and some soap. Oh no, I thought not again, a scrubbing with a beating. They told me they would help cleanse me for the master's will and I should *sing praises* as they do so.

The ladies scrubbed and scrubbed on me until I felt my skin would peel off, the whole time singing and saying all kinds of things like 'hallelujah', and 'praise God', and so many others things my head began to swim from dizziness and pain. I began to cry, it was starting to sting. It felt like they scrubbed me for hours, but I know it had to only be a few minutes because the water was not yet cold and it was slightly soothing when they rinsed me off. The taller lady motioned for me to get out of the tub to be dried off. I got up and out of the tub and felt sore and stiff and humiliated as they began to dry me off and wrapped me in a towel and told me to sit and wait for the air to clear and they would say a prayer for my total submission to God's will.

It was all so confusing as I tried to battle what I was thinking might be happening, but I was not sure, I was after all just still a child, and not even had my period yet, so I was not a woman, and the rumors of tales of sexuality and sex that was to be within the bounds of marriage, I had never known much of anything about except stories I overheard. But I was always under the assumption that one could not be able to do that as a kid. This truly could not be what was about to happen, I thought to myself, I was not yet a woman in full bloom? They began to put some oily scented lotion on my skin and rubbed it in all over, I was feeling very gross and sick to my stomach. I began to shake, and the lady combing the tangles out of my hair said, "You are trembling because you are being filled with the *Holy Spirit* in preparation for your calling". I wanted to cry out in protest and say, "I was actually trembling because I was so scared and was really wishing I were dead instead of having two crazy woman give me a bath and touch me in a manner that felt horrid".

The shorter lady continued to brush my hair as the other taller one decided to dress me in soft white silk and linen slip and dress. I have to admit the dress did feel soft and nice after the clothing I had been forced to wear over the last few months. They smelled of fabric softener and not the old stuffy musty smell of the dorms' closets and stinky shoes. It had just struck me as they had finished dressing me and my hair was dry, what the other sisters had said must be true, my time had come, and it was evident there was no escaping this doom. My heart sank, and I wanted to die, right then, right there, death would be my only salvation. That day I would learn ultimate submission of will, all in the name of *self-sacrifice* to their God.

The ladies escorted me back to the main room and had me sit on the couch. Then one of them went to the kitchen and reappeared with a glass of ice and a soda pop in hand. I was a bit excited since I had not seen or tasted any carbonated beverage in months. That excitement dissipated quickly, when I realized, they were only being kind because something evil was about to embark on my life. They then once again left me alone and I could hear a key turn in the lock of the door and the tumbler to the dead bolt engage was sealing my fate. I sat there drinking the soda and burping the alphabet to pass the time, hoping perhaps I could wake up from this and realize it was all a nightmare. What had my mother done to me, by leaving me here for this to happen? She betrayed me. I thought a girl's mother was supposed to direct and guide her. I had never felt so abandoned and thrown to the wolves in my life. I began to cry and at the same time wondered why since it seemed no one was listening to me and no one was seeing my tears, or at least no one that cared. I became angry inside and cursed my mother.

You walked away,

You didn't care.

That it was me,

You left standing there.

I reached out to you,

You looked away,

I said good-bye,

Yet begged you stay.

My heart now aches,

Broken in two.

Why pray tell,

I would never do this to you.

Leave you alone,

To feel the pain,

Of emptiness,

And bitter distain.

For my will did cave,

Now I have no more.

You've taken It from me,

My heart a closed door.

I have built my wall,

A fortress none dare get in.

Filled with anger and pain,

That's bottled within.

If you should return,

When saving my soul done.

To tear down these walls,

The Battle's just begun.

I was startled when I heard the door unlock, it frightened me enough I almost felt I would pee right there on the couch. The door came opened and there stood Brother Mack and another woman I had never laid eyes on before. She looked at Brother Mack and said, "this is the one you had chosen, I hope you are pleased and blessed". I felt my feet rise up like a lump in my throat as he answered her and said, "Yes, she is perfect and ready. "Bring her to me when I call for her". Then he went into the bedroom and shut the door.

The lady came and sat next to me, and told me her name was Sister Thelma, and said, "I should be submissive and let the will of God happen tonight". Then Brother Mack called out for me, and I was escorted to the door, shoved in and I heard the door shut behind me, and felt the life drain out of me completely and stood there horrified.

I was then touched, fondled, abused and tortured sexually in a manner that I cannot elaborate on without finding myself totally revolted and in tears to this day. I remember fighting and Brother Mack holding me down and telling me that I should not let the devil in me fight him. He was so strong and I was so weak, I had succumbed to his will. I am not sure how many hours I was put through this punishment and abuse. After a while the pain was so immense, the feeling was so vile I began to drift in and out. I am not sure if I had totally passed out or what because the next thing I recalled was lying there alone, curled up in a ball, shivering. I felt so sick I threw up in the bed but was in too much pain to even move. I cried myself to sleep.

-9-

I was presented, used, then sent back to the bunkhouse, never to speak of the happenings again, for fear of reprisal or lockdown. I spent numerous hours just sitting in the communal restroom vomiting and crying, pained and bleeding, feeling violated of any sense of self. Death would have been a reprise.

To this day, the memories of that event bring nausea to my lips, and they purse with anger. I spoke of it to no one, for fear of the lockdown room, which was a small closet, where non-submissive girls were forced to stay in total darkness, their own filth and excrement encompassing them as they harbor there for days, being allowed only an opening of the door to receive minimal food waste scraped from the plates of Elders, as the staff were so pompously named. In my silence, I remained a boiling kettle within, torn between understanding what I felt and succumbed to what I had become at their hands. For what was taken from me at that time, was something I had always felt should only be given at will to the one we choose to love.

Several more times over the next few weeks I was presented to that vile man, only to be scorned later for my defiance. I was so repulsed by his touch and perverted kissing and fondling that I would slap, scratch and bite him only to be tied down and forced to submit to any of his requests and vile perversions. I had grown tired of being beaten and treated harshly so to save myself from abuse, I gave in to will and figured I had better just let things happen. It seemed as if the more I fought the more Brother Mack was turned on and called for me to be brought to the cottage. I then began to think perhaps if I did not fight and was no longer a challenge to get to submit the sooner I would be replaced. I would be freed from this learning process.

Each time Brother Mack was finished with me, I was returned back to the dormitory and told to never speak of any of the happenings or surely God would punish me. At a young age and out of fear, I complied and spoke to no one about it. I would return to my bunk and cry. There were times when I felt so disgusted and dirty and in pain I was too numb to even shed a tear.

Eventually I was replaced by another, although I felt for her impending doom, I was relieved that my purpose had been suited, and I was considered submissive and no longer in need of 'lessons'. Filled with hatred so deep, I decided I must play this game, and pray for release from this living hell.

I never spoke of this happening to my mother or anyone else until a few decades later. Not that she would believe it anyway. Over the years, I have always wondered how many of us girls there were that had been *chosen for the calling* to submit to the servant of God. I have chosen to relive and vent through poetry, and make it my release from the pain that burdens me as they sit free and walk among us; still revered as *good servants* of their God.

To have felt me inside, I was but a dead soul,

Longing for relief, I wished only to be whole.

I scrubbed my surface, with fierceness in vain,

Cleansed outside, yet loathe the filth of inner pain.

Show no reason, that I must live,

I wanted not to go on, not to forgive.

Youth and innocence did flee,

From that moment, I was no longer ‘me’.

Cloaked in white, as new fallen snow,

My will and identity no more to know.

Surrendered and broken, I had to give away,

The very part of me, I shall take back one day.

Soul stolen, but mind still my gift,

I lingered only to exist, one day this would lift.

I would become strong, when no longer a pawn.

Neither you nor I knowing, the entity to spawn.

I cannot get back all that's been taken from me,

I have left that up to the powers that be.

For one day in Hell they shall see,

That will be their destiny.

I did eventually escape the majority of the abuse that had befallen me in the past by the staff, with the arrival of my mother, to the compound as an employer of theirs. I was not sure why she came to work there. Even though she had come, I was not allowed to live in the staff apartment dorms with her. She was told I was still rebellious and must remain in the reform dormitory. I would be only feet away from my mother and my little sister several times a day and was not allowed to acknowledge them as my family. My sister was too young and filled with tales of how evil and unruly I had allegedly become that she was forbidden to have communication with me unless regulated with staff and only a brief hello and I love you. She hung out with the other staff kids who never knew the horrors within the dorm, I could not quite understand how my own mother could be as evil as these people or was she just as naive as the many visitors that came to attend Sunday services and pour their money into the offering plates as Brother Mack would beg and tell them that the homes were in need of money to pay to keep the sinful wayward boys and girls off the streets of a world destined for destruction with the coming of the rapture. To this date, I do not think she is aware of all their misleading and secret escapades with wards once in their care for reformation. I was told that I shall never speak of the happenings to my mother, or I would be harshly punished by death or the wrath of God in Hell. A few months later I am not sure what happened, and I had heard my mother arguing with a few staff members and the next thing I knew she was packing to leave and I was getting to go with her. I did not ask questions, I just packed and left with her. I did not know where we were headed. I had heard her talking on a pay phone to someone and had said something about heading to Texas to a job she was offered. When we did arrive there I found out she had sought employment with another organization with the same strictness and twisted fundamentalist ideals.

I felt then either she was losing her mind, or was truly seeking answers to fill a void she had developed. Desiring to find solace in the seeking out a purer form of life pleasing to the God she served. Still defiant in thought, I rebelled even more. In her eyes and the eyes of others with the same ideals, I was but a tool of the Devil lost and doomed. I could do nothing pleasing or right. I wanted so much to be free of this religious nightmare that I was growing very angry with this God they worshipped and became even more defiant that I had in the past. I was filled with so much hate that I was like a ticking time bomb just waiting to explode into any rebellious behavior I could. I was determined to intentionally look for reasons to anger everyone around me. The whole time I was rebelling I was losing a bit of myself and forgetting who I was, even I did not like what I saw in myself. I would lay in bed at night and cry myself to sleep, hoping one day that maybe, just maybe I would wake up from this year long nightmare, and I would be back in my bed in

Michigan, and back where I knew the people were not as crazy as they were here.

Can you hear me crying inside?

Do you envision the tears that fall on the cheeks of
my soul?

The mere existence of who I am slowly fading,

Creating within itself a pain and I cannot fathom
survival.

For it draws from me the last of breath I seek for life.

Last breath gone, I am now as but a shell,

Robotic in nature as do the peers that encompass
me,

We together in a twisted yet, programmed manner

Perform as if to be circus monkeys on display

In a carnival of theological ideology.

The dance we so delicately set upon the soles of our feet

Are but mere movements from one place to another

Performing tasks at hand for the grand master of this carnival.

The songs upon our tongue, are but mere words,

Flowing in synchronized tune as if to be a music grinder.

Wound to entertain the wishes of the viewer.

In hopes for a reward in heaven so graciously bestowed, disguised,

As a coin to be tossed upon our begging tin.

Some moments I perceived myself as if to be the accordion held by a primate.

Weaving in and out playing a tune that some feel amusing and others

But wounding to the ears.

How doth one become so consumed with a life so
perplexed, so freely giving in,

So bound by submission, that they lower themselves
to demeaning.

Survival, reprieve, rescue from perils so clearly stated
as if they become reality.

Mind so compromising and confused, one goes on,
and secretly holds out for hope.

The difference between Texas and Louisiana was that I was on the other side of the situation. I was not thrust into the reformatory dorms of the compound at first. I was with my mother and my sister, living in a trailer at the far end of the compound, with the rest of the staff. I had thought to myself perhaps this is not too bad and I only had a few more years to go and I could leave this place and no one could stop me. I participated in the usual activities with other staff members kids, and then there was BOY. I of course like any typical girl thought it cute when a boy looked at me, or said hello. In my mother's eyes it meant that I was soliciting sex and doomed to hell as a whore. She even called me a tramp on numerous occasions whenever I even looked at a boy. I truly wonder is this because she had not remarried after divorcing my father and being I doubt any other man would be willing to share a life with someone that was so anal retentive and filled with animosity. I could never picture my mother being in a household with a man when she must always be in control, and under the fundamentalist belief system she partook of, a woman that is married must be submissive and my mother was a person that just could not give up her overbearing and controlling nature.

I managed to last about a month, then sure enough, my mother thought I was tampering with the devil because I actually said hello and laughed with one of the boys who was telling a joke. I did not even like the boy, the joke was funny, and I laughed.

That did not matter. That day she warned me that I was going to wind up in the reform dormitory with the other girls if I did not behave. I knew I was in trouble and had to get out of this place. I had to somehow run away and hunt for my father, who probably did not know where I was. I had worked sometimes in the local "store" as they call it where staff could buy some things brought to the compound from the outside world. So I knew this was perhaps my opportunity to make a means for escape.

I was asked to watch the register for the store manager while he went to get some more supplies from off the back of his pickup truck, and when he did I saw my opportunity to steal a few dollars to take and I would tell him I felt ill and had to go home, and would make a b-line for the fence and get over it and flee. This fence was the same as it was on the compound in Louisiana with the exception that it was 6 feet instead of 8 feet and the barbed wire atop it was missing in a few places behind one of the buildings. I was going to run away and try to use the money to eat and then hitchhike out of the state. Being so young and naive I did not realize how far Texas was from Michigan, and that most people would turn a kid in for hitchhiking along a rural highway. That lack of knowledge did not matter anyway. Unknown to me, my mother had made plans in advance to have me placed in the dormitory because I was in her words, "a whore in the making", all because I communicated with a boy and nothing more.

-10-

Back behind the walls of a fundamentalist kiddies' prison I went. Crap! I was doomed to unknown circumstances once again. This time I was a year older and at least a year wiser to what is expected of me, and I would just have to try my hardest to be as well behaved as possible, despite the fact I had a mind and a will of my own. I was torn between the decision as to whether I would do my best to be a nightmare to everyone around or should I conform and play the game again. I had already survived what I thought was the cruelest punishment in Louisiana that a kid could endure, what else could they throw at me that could be any more miserable than that?

The Rebekah Dormitory was not as bad as the one in Louisiana dorm. This dorm was full of three to four girl rooms with a shared bathroom between every set of two rooms. We had decorative spreads on regular beds, and a dresser and closets. I figured they had to make them look nice considering they were always having donors tour the place to entice large contributions to their cause. However each window was equipped with an alarm system and every dresser was scrutinized as to its contents, and the clothing was an ugly uniform, which was a fashion alarm in any country! The exterior of the dorm was surrounded by an additional fence covered in barbed wire and even taller than the fence surrounding the whole compound. Nothing says "I love you and care about you" better than barbed wire and electricity!

At the end of each long hallway of about 40 rooms, there was a laundry room, confinement rooms and prayer hall. The prayer hall and confinement rooms of course were never part of the tours with visitors, and I am sure if they were included, they would have been shut down or lost plenty of donations. They had a den at the other end with a few couches that we girls were not allowed to sit on, except Sundays after Church to look good for tourists. We were required to memorize answers on what we thought of our lives at the dorm, in case anyone asked us while touring the place.

Our uniforms were either navy blue or bright red skirts with elastic waist bands so one size fit all. Either almost falling off or almost squeezed into. We had red or blue plaid gingham shirts to match fitting about as poorly, and a blue or red scar to tie around our necks to cover any flesh showing between the collar and chin. Some days we were permitted to wear a uniform style bow tie with our blouses when we went to school. Either accompaniment to our uniform did nothing for the appearance and I thought we all looked like retarded fools.

I hated that uniform so much, especially the red one since it made me feel like I was wearing a red picnic tablecloth. When we were not in uniform and working the farm we had to wear pleated culottes that went below our knees and were itchy and hot. At least with a skirt you had some air flow. Texas was awful hot so when you add a skirt over a slip and undergarments one got pretty toasted in the summer.

The days I did like the most were when we had the opportunity to be sent in groups to the inter-coastal waterway to fish for food. Every Sunday they served fresh friend speckled brown trout, and between the boys' and girls' homes we had to catch enough to cook it for us and the visitors. The boys from the boys' home did most of the catching, but sometimes we girls had to help out. We were shipped to stay for a few days at a time to shacks on the coast. We would fish for the three days and swim in the water to cool off or wash the sweat off of us. There was an outhouse as a bathroom and jugs of water to drink and we had packed sandwiches in coolers. There was no running water or electricity for the three day duration. I actually enjoyed it, because while fishing there was no preaching and scripture memorizing and mental torture. We would fish and no one would bother us to pump us for a daily memorization of some scripture. We got to sleep a whole eight hour night. It was nice to enjoy the quiet.

It seemed much nicer than past, so I figured I would give it a try. Once again I will play along and make the best of it and let them think they changed me, and keep my true self hidden inside. I tried my best and gave in to my weakness of wanting to be myself on occasion.

I sang the songs and walked the walk as they demanded, to the point I was near insane with rebellion and a desire to break free of the bullshit. They had so many songs we always had to sing while we worked, to show an outward sign of being content in following the labors of God in support of the compound community. I used to hum along and actually instead of singing the words they were signing, I would sing the words to the songs I wrote myself to ease the stress of such a twisted group of people. One time while I was working in one of the gardens alone, I did not notice that someone was close by as I bellowed out my own written words to the tune of their songs.

For that childish stunt, I spent four hours kneeling on a tile floor with a thin layer of rock salt that was spread out and meant for me to kneel on. A pencil was placed between my knees lengthwise so I could not try and shift the balance from one knee to the other to relieve pain or alternate my weight. The salt was coarse and would cut into my knees. I had to recite certain phrases referenced to my behaviors that led me to this punishment. Every time I moved or adjusted, quoting the required penance, "Lord forgive my unworthy sinful ways, for I am but a sinner gone astray from your fold", the salt would grind into my skin and burn. But I had to keep kneeling, I had to not let them break me down and give up, just four hours, and it would be over. I could barely stand up when I had finished my punishment. My knees swelled, and all they would allow was alcohol to cleanse my knees. I don't know about you, but believe it or not salt was not as painful as alcohol on an open wound. I had to wearily suck it up and just learn to be more careful and not get caught singing that loudly tunes that showed signs of rebellion.

I look back and remember, even then, although my knees bled and hurt and my throat was hoarse from quoting for four hours, and know some things in life are well worth the pain. That was one of the 'well worth it' moments. For in not breaking and giving up, they did not get the chance to beat me with a board until I couldn't sit. Yet I still wonder to myself, what the heck were these people doing with rock salt in southern Texas anyway, it never snows there? The only big storms I remember were the hurricanes I created. One of the songs that I wrote after the salt punishment and one that landed me in even more trouble was this;

I walk among the nuts and wonder to myself

Are they as crazy in the eyes of others as they appear to me?

We shout praise at every beckoned call

Just what is their meaning of "Glory Be"?

Drag me from my sleep so early

Milk a cow then shovel poo

As if it couldn't wait

"Glory Be" I have much better things to do.

Picking cotton until my fingers bleed

To send out to the mill

Baking in the hot Texas sun

"Glory Be" I think I am getting ill.

Assembly lines just to eat

Food we cooked in kettles the size of pools

We feed the many people

"Glory Be" such a gathering of fools.

Now it's worship time

How many hours kneeling in prayer,

Will be my punishment today

"Glory Be" did anyone really care?

I play my game, and plan my escape

You will not own my mind

One day you will see

"Glory Be" I will leave this all behind!

As a new teen, I figured since it contained their most commonly used statement, "Glory Be", that it would not mean, "Oh Shit" for me. Yet another immature though gone awry. That song bit me in the ass a few more times over a few months when I was under the assumption no one could hear me singing it aloud. One time in the wee hours of the morning while shoveling cow crap I belted it out loudly, knowing I shouldn't have, but I just could not resist rebellion against something I did not believe was right. I did not believe this God they worshipped was as unforgiving, and so harsh to send me to a flaming pit of fire when I die for singing such a thing.

I awaited my punishment and felt I would survive it smugly and remain proud of my misbehavior. That was until I experienced their version of discipline for the second offence of singing a song of mockery or worldliness. I was forced to stand upon a 2x4 piece of wood on the floor and balance for two hours without wobbling or losing my footing, and falling off. I lasted about thirty minutes before my toes started tingling and my legs were hurting from muscles tensing and trying to keep balance, then I fell to the floor. I was told either my time was to start over or I could just have a paddling instead. Acrobatics was not a skill I perfected so I just opted for the beating because I knew it was to follow anyway. They would always come up with a reason to paddle you even if you stood there on the 2x4 for the duration of the four hours. As defiantly as I could I took that beating and walked away mouthing off to the staff in charge.

The beatings, or as they referred to them like so many other fundamentalist freaks do, a way of making the devil flee from one's soul, were no picnic themselves. Now I am a firm believer in corporal punishment in moderation when no other alternative form of discipline gains positive results, but beating someone by exposing their bare posterior and smacking it with a board until welts or blood is drawn to the surface as they are held down by one or more other individuals is hardly appropriate. After a few of them I had wished so many times we were in Alaska so I could go sit in a snow drift and put the fire on my ass out. Where was the Geneva Convention then? Enemy combatants were protected then too were they not? Well at least the elders there thought I was the enemy at times, when they were not referring me to a spawn of Satan. Brother Wiley C., the director of the dorms referred to anyone not following the "will of God" as spawns of the devil.

The more I tried to be like the others the more I found myself riding an invisible fence between an earthly heaven and living hell. To be deprived of commonalities of most American households and replacing them with only Fundamentalist-based propaganda is just wrong. All conduct and affiliations were only as dictated by the leader of the organization. I knew I had to somehow be removed from this situation, and out of juvenile naivety I chose to rebel against their religious teachings and break every rule they had established as if to have a mental list, scrolling down it, committing one after another violation of their sacredness.

-11-

Over time I found myself in quite a decisive pickle. I could never seem to make up my mind. I knew I could act my way through this, but also I had such a strong will to be myself. I just could not decide which path to take. Shall I conform, shall I play a role as to appear conforming, or shall I rebel even more so they feel they cannot break me? I chose the latter in the beginning, to find myself experiencing the *hole* in the *hallway of prayer.* Now that was an experience I am quite sure most prisoners of war can relate to in one aspect or another. My first tour of the *hallway of prayer* and the *hole*, one would think would have been enough, but no, not for me, I relished the self glory of self will and arrogance within myself to visit it numerous times over several months.

What was the *hole* and *hall of prayer* you ask? I shall tell you what they wished it to be, and what I perceived it to be for me.

Within the dormitory where I was placed to be reformed from my sinful ways, there was a hall: narrow, donned with fading gray paint and worn carpet from where many loyal supporters to the cause, had knelt reverently in prayer for the souls that were to pass through it. In that hall were also two doors, both of which contained a keyed deadbolt, and opened up a deep dark space approximately the size of a walk-in closet, with no light, but a loud speaker mounted midway up the interior wall.

No ventilation and no escape. It smelled of human sweat, despair and defeat blended with a sense of inevitable demise. The captors which they were meant to contain must rely on the limited means and supplies intended to create a submissive spirit. One tattered blanket, too small to cover a toddler properly, a five gallon bucket with a lid and a roll of the roughest toilet tissue one could only relate to when using a nineteenth century outhouse and a dried out corncob.

This surely was not the Ramada Inn! The doors were opened just long enough to thrust in a plate of food cold and stagnated by hours of delay, three times a day, the bucket to be used as a restroom, and emptied only upon compliance in quoting scriptures or prayers played repeatedly over the speakers, round the clock on cycles, and one was not allowed to speak except to quote what was demanded.

The staff thought it to be a means of breaking ones ill will and defiant spirit by exposing them to harsh conditions and repeated brainwashing to create conformity and submission. They felt that if a person was left there long enough they would eventually give in and comply. The usual stay was 5 days to a week or until one screamed out and begged in repentance of their evil ways and would confess their sins and beg to the people on the other side of the door praying, to pray for them. Then they must pledge allegiance to God and the staff, and usually were relieved of their bondage and allowed to return to their dorm rooms, restricted and with a leader. A leader was another girl in the dorm already brainwashed into total conformity and could not process a thought of their own without the influence of the teachings crammed into their heads. So restriction was like being around a prison warden twenty-four seven.

What I felt inside was that it was by-far different in many ways. Perhaps that is because I found myself in there so many times I had become accustomed to the solitude. It became my imaginary retreat for which I could flee. I knew that if I did not comply with their demands and survive emotionally, the 7 days each visit deemed the maximum stay, I would be freed for a brief period of weeks.

I spent my first few times in the smaller confinement rooms, 'hole one' as it was called. I was first forced to change into a nightgown, and then sent to start my sentence. The door closed being me, and I thought to myself, I will find a way to make the best of this and not conform, and not give in. I was determined not to throw myself upon the mercy of the idiots on the other side of the door and beg them for anything. They were not better than I, and I would NOT give in. I had been sitting on the foam mat on the floor not much longer than about ten minutes before the speaker above my head started bellowing preaching and prayers over and over again in the pitch dark. I felt around for the toilet tissue set atop the five gallon bucket that was to be my makeshift toilet and immediately made a primitive set of ear plugs to drown out the noise.

I learned to count the hours by the cycles of the near warped recordings being played. Every sermon would be followed by a few songs and long prayers, which I estimated was an hour. Then I knew girls were sent to pray on the hall every four hours, so I could calculate a day pretty easily. When followers of the compound's beliefs felt the need to pray once again, as they kneeled along the hall, I would hum to myself old nursery rhymes grandma taught me as a small child to drown them out. Sometimes I would sing nursery rhymes out loud just to make them mad and be defiant. The louder I hummed, the louder they yelled out for God to rebuke the demons in me. At times it became amusing.

They would bring small rations of bread and peanut butter and a paper cup of water for meals to me. They would open the door and shove it in and shut and lock the door real fast. I didn't like the crap meals so to survive I would pass time by pretending that I was a queen upon a throne and it was a royal meal. The peanut butter was steak and the stale bread was the finest rolls with butter and jelly. That got tiring quickly, and I just ate it and usually went back to sleep with my ear plugs in. After several times in the hole for the duration of seven day stints

I did decide it was in my best interest to not press my luck and behave just enough to not wind up in there again. It was getting close to winter time and cooler months and the hole was not heated, and I didn't want to freeze in there. Besides, after a few days in there with no bath even you start smelling bad to yourself, and add the stench of a bucket for a bathroom, one can only take so much.

One time I was even lucky enough to get put into 'hole two'. This was much nicer! It was actually a room with a bathroom. The bed was a regular twin mattress on the floor with a sheet on it and the blanket was full sized. The room was big enough I could move and walk around in the dark. I had moved to uptown punishment! The bathroom had a really dim light that was about as bright as a night light, the faucet handles had been removed but the toilet worked. It was so well equipped with good sound effects, having two speakers to preach at me all day and night! I lasted a whole seven days in there with no sweat, I took the sheet off the bed and took water from the back tank of the toilet to wash up daily and hurried and put the sheet back on the bed before meal rations were brought in to me. I would walk around in circles touching the walls to keep sense of the room, and pass time. Of course I had earplugs I made again to avoid being annoyed by the noise. I was not going to cave in and let them win. I did my seven days defiantly.

I knew their only purpose for forcing someone to endure those conditions was to create a sense of fear in me. They wanted to control me and brainwash me by making me afraid. I was not going to let them do that. I would not fear them. Although things or events in life may leave me with a sense of unrest, There is only one thing I fear, and that is the wrath of the real God, not the "God" they portrayed I should fear. Fear in itself can become a prison within our minds harboring discomfort. Fear was something I began to learn I could control, for fear in itself to me had become but a mere shadow of nothingness once I discovered I had the power of self-will to rid it from my thoughts. Fear is but a mere ghost, it does not exist, except our fear of our creator, and that fear is dispelled through our belief in His goodness.

A shadow,

A cloud.

Weighing down,

Upon my mind

Griping firmly,

No release.

Pressure strong,

Tight the bind.

Taken hold,

Separating my soul.

Blinding my view,

Where do I turn.

Run away,

Cannot hide.

Your there,

Freedom I yearn.

I wake,

I find.

Pain within,

Wonder why.

I sleep,

I cry.

Let go of me,

I need to fly.

Flee I must,

Go I will.

One day I find.

What I need most.

Release from you,

I seek to hold,

My fright be gone,

Leave, MY FEAR, MY GHOST.

Over the weeks when I along with others were called upon to go to the hall of prayer and pray for the lost souls behind the doors, I knew everyone closed their eyes during prayer, so I would sneak parts of lunchmeat and things down the hall with me to push under the doors to the victims behind them, hoping to let them know that someone understood them on the outside. On a few occasions when I knew someone should not have been sent there, I would ask a leader if I could spend extra time praying for them, and was usually grated time to alone. I then made sure to sneak extras to pass under the door that had only about an inch and a half gap to push things thru. That is how I met my friend Terry. After she was let out of there we soon became friends. She and I felt the same way about this crazy place and were going to help each other survive and get through it together.

-12-

Terry and I found it was quite a bit easier to survive walking amongst the freaks if we created a circus of our own. We would make the best of every moment we could until we were freed from our prison of fundamentalist bondage. She was a spirited rebel with a love for writing, and we shared so many like ideals. We made a pact one morning, that whenever one of us had been freed from this living hell, that we would find a way to keep in touch with each other. Although that promise was meant, secretly neither of us wanted the other to part this place, because we were each other's coping mechanism.

Our rooms were separated by a bathroom, we took advantage of every chance we could to compare our days or plan to do things together. Even if it meant the worst of chores, we would volunteer to do them when others wouldn't just to be together. Even if it meant peeling potatoes for 6 hours and until blisters rose on our fingers, or shoveling cow crap until we were near vomiting from the smell, it didn't matter because we could laugh and know that we were not alone. We had each other. Two young girls trapped in a world where we didn't belong. Nothing seemed as bad as long as we didn't have to do it alone. Of course even punishments were not bad as long as we had battle scars to compare. We actually managed not to get into too much trouble, because we did not want to end up being separated. The notes we would leave being the washing machine unsigned for each other were like finding hidden treasures.

The staff discouraged close friendships between girls, they were afraid it might lead to homosexual relationships, because girls were not supposed to be too close. I guess they had a different value system on a friendship. Closeness between friends had nothing to do with physical attractions. Surely one was definitely going to burn in hell if they were close enough to hug and be as close as we were, so we were forced to hide our friendship as much as we could, to the point we even planned picking fights with each other and bickering in front of staff to make them think we had a conflict with each other. When two girls had conflicts with each other, they were usually forced to work together on chores isolated from the rest of the group to work through their issues, and this was a perfect way for us to have time to spend without the staff bugging us.

One time we were having a good old time washing some goats and having such a laugh we almost got caught. About the time staff was close enough we had to act like the reason we were totally soaked was not because we were playing around but pretended we were mad and fighting over who was to wash and who was to rinse, so we started throwing things at each other and yelling. We were both then harshly punished to two weeks of working together alone, cleaning the goat pens. It was a stinky job but at least we knew it meant two more weeks to hang out and share stories about our room leaders and their psycho dedication to the fundamentalist cause. We had made secret nicknames for all the staff we hated. We would sing using the handles of the shovels we used to scoop out the stalls as microphones and make fun of the music we were forced to sing. Laughter was our medicine, our cure for the ailing moments during the week we were forced to endure. Life was looking up.

We would rush through our chores as fast as we could then lay in the hay, with pieces of straw hanging out of our mouths, complaining that the hay had itched our bare legs and sharing dreams and plans for our futures. I was going to be a famous writer and one day tell the world my stories and memories of this hell hole we were trapped in. Terry was going to be a famous singer and actress and marry a rich guy and have loads of kids. We would laugh and talk about how we would swear to never sing the songs we had to here, and would never force our kids to ever live like this, and they could have soda pop and chips and watch television or listen to rock and roll. We were going to be rebels clean to the bone. To us that was the ultimate sin that would surely land us in hell. Then we would laugh and decide who would be responsible for filling our coffins with ice. Oh the memories we shared! I can remember them as if they were yesterday.

The tales of adventures we dreamed, we shared, the plans to escape and run wild and free along the ocean, collecting shells. In our minds it was so real we could almost smell the salty air and feel the sand beneath our toes. The only disappointing moments were when our dreams were interrupted by a supper bell or staff. Then reality set in and we were snapped back into reality like a boomerang hitting us in the forehead. Then one day it happened.

Like a tornado spinning through a prairie field disrupting the balance of nature that evil staff member appeared from around the corner and caught us lying on the hay with our heads on each other's shoulders,; holding hands like sisters, laughing and all hell broke loose and accusations flew like wildfire through a dry forest. We were both called into Brother C's office, and we knew to land in front of his desk meant a good paddling, isolation, or worse… banned from communicating with each other and punished for being worldly, being lesbians! To think we were not even quite sure what a lesbian does! We were after all sheltered from much social knowledge of the secular world how would we know we did anything wrong morally. We were almost convinced we must be, we did get caught holding hands after all. Oh my! Surely we were doomed for Hell! I hope they have ice machines in hell because I would probably be in the hottest part for this one.

Did God really hate us because we shared a kiss once, that we were allowed to be caught just innocently laughing and holding hands? I hardly think that is even in the same category of sins. We were banned from any contact, and Terry was moved to the first floor of the dormitory. We would get to see each other only in passing through the halls and it was hard to sneak a peek and a smile, most often we could not. But we still had our secret spot behind the washing machines to leave notes for each other. Then one day I did not see Terry standing at her usual spot in line, and wondered where she was. I knew I just had to get to the washing machine to look behind it and see if I could find a note. I needed to know something. I could not find my best buddy, the only person here that understood me and felt the same way, I was lost. A few hours passed and I had near given myself whiplash from searching over my shoulder, hoping to see her somewhere, anywhere and I was beginning to feel a sense of panic and fear that what if something bad had happened and they had hurt her.

When I finally had an opportunity to get away from the group I made a mad dash to the washing machines in the laundry room, like a rabid mutt running from an animal control officer. I was nearly out of breath when I got to there and saw a note, sighed and snatched it up and headed straight to the bathroom, so I could hide and read it. As I read the message, it was like feeling a sharpened arrow piercing clean through my soul. Terry wrote that her parents had decided to come and get her, they were arriving today and she was packed up and told she could not talk to anyone or say good-bye, she left a phone number on the note and told me when I was finally free, to call her so we could reconnect and be together again even if only by phone or letters until we both were adults.

I truly felt like a part of me died that day. There was only one person in the world that understood me, my dreams, my hopes and wishes, and now they were yanked away from me. The thought of surviving this place without her was like a nightmare and I sat there and cried for what seemed like hours, and just told everyone that bugged me I had the flu. I just wanted everyone to go away and stay away. I wanted to have a moment alone.

Eventually things got easier and whenever I missed terry, I would close my eyes and remember our laughs together and looked forward to the chance to talk to her again. I memorized her number and remembered her face, her laugh and carried it in my heart every day. One day we would be a part of each other's lives again, one day.

-13-

The day came for me to leave the main compound. I was to be sent as part of 'God's Will' to another extension of the sect. I was called into the main office and told I would be going to a place I would enjoy and I could be of great help. Pleasant Valley was my new location, where I would work the kitchens for seniors and visiting elderly who had contributed their estates upon death to the cause. I would help cook and clean up and then have freedom to roam the property. So this sounded great and I was relieved that I had my escape I would get there and plan my means of fleeing. WRONG!

Upon my arrival, of course there was no gate or guard shack, just a sign pointing down a road. It seemed like we had driven down a dirt road for at least five minutes. I looked out the windows of the van, back and forth on both sides, and all I could see were rows and rows of trees, hundreds of them. I saw orange trees to my left and grapefruit trees to my right. I love oranges and grapefruit. This was going to be nice. No fences, no barbed wire, and trees of fruit for miles and miles. Fruit for as far as the eye could see!

The van stopped right in front of a large plantation type house that was like a picture I saw on a book cover a long time ago. I got out and was immediately greeted by a tall husky man in a suit and toting a Bible under his right arm, and a smirk on his face. What's with these people that they feel the need to tote around large print King James versions of the Bible? He welcomed me and told me to get settled and have a look around and he would have Janice meet with me and get me settled into where I would work and what was expected of me. I was shown to a stairway and told my room was the last door on the right, so I went up the stairs and made my way down the hall.

I opened the door and saw a room that was bigger than any bedroom I had ever laid eyes on. This was far more adequate than the previous accommodations I had been given over the years. It had a big bed that I could lay any direction on and never have to worry about my feet hanging off the end.

There was a dresser that was tall and another long dresser that had a mirror on it almost as long as the bed. There was an old desk with some paper and an ink pen too. There were two doors. The first one I opened was a bathroom. I had a bathroom all my own and a nice big tub with bear claw feet to soak in! No waiting in line and no one barging in on me or staring at me telling me my time was up. The other was a closet that was almost as big as the bathroom. I was beginning to really like this place.

There were several windows covered with white curtains, and I looked out the one by the bed and I saw trees and a walkway and picnic tables, then I ran to look out the other and saw several small cottages in a row and older people walking around. I sat back down for a moment and thought this was so much nicer than the past.

Perhaps these people here are not as bad as everyone else I had ever met in this nutty organization. I closed my eyes for a moment and took a deep breath in. I could smell the fragrance of fresh flowers so I opened my eyes and noticed a vase on the night stand had fresh cut flowers in it. This was wonderful, I thought to myself. Eventually I would learn the price I would be expected to pay for this luxury.

I unpacked my belongings and decided to take a stroll. Downstairs was a foyer, and the main room was remodeled into a dining hall and meeting room and a very large kitchen at the far end. I went outside to have a good look around before I would be interrupted to learn what my duties were to be. It was warm out and the sunshine felt great on my face as I walked around. The seniors all greeted me nicely and shook my hand and one lady placed a few hard candies in my palm. I had not indulged in any candy in so long. I unwrapped one and placed it in my mouth. It was so good, I thanked and hugged her. She had no idea how much I loved it.

I heard someone call my name, and turned around in time to see that Bible toting weirdo that's look gave me the creeps walking towards me with a lady I assumed correctly to be Janice. He introduced her then walked away. As he was leaving Janice mumbled under her breath, "Insufferable asshole", and I knew I was going to like her from that moment on.

She walked along with me for a bit, and explained to me I was to get up early and cook for the seniors that live here. I would cook them three meals a day and two on Sundays and wash all the dishes and clean up the dining room. She was in charge of cleaning the floors and the seniors' laundry and cottage cleanup, but would help me the first few days to learn the routines.

She explained that the seniors that lived in the cottages were at one time well-to-do people, who upon retirement's latter years had chosen to endow all of their worldly possessions to the organization. They chose to dedicate their final moments in tribute to God, devotions, scripture reading, preaching and prayer. She told me it was not too bad as long as I made sure to try and never be caught alone with Brother Al. I inquired further and she refused to elaborate. I didn't want to push it too much for fear of being sent back up North to the main compound again.

I would cook for twenty-seven seniors and eight staff daily including myself. Talk about a crash course in cooking! At least a menu and all recipes were provided in a manual that was there for me to follow. I just had to follow what directions there were and stick to the strict menu and then clean everything up when each meal was done. This would be like cooking for a family, which I had never done, just multiplied a few extra times. The supplies were provided by a person who ordered things weekly from town, so I would not have to worry about not having what I needed for the menu.

I took the book to my room with me to study it before the next day, and collected an orange sitting in a bowl on my way there. I fell asleep somewhere between the section telling me how to make oatmeal a gallon at a time and how to not make lumpy gravy, because that's the last I remembered before someone knocked on my door and said "rise and shine, we have to be working at five".

Off to the kitchen I went. First thing was to cook and then set the table placements and ring the breakfast bell all before 7am. That was like running a marathon and never leaving the room. The seniors all came in and seated themselves and Brother Al read a devotional and blessed the morning meal. No sooner than he had uttered the "Amen", a herd of fake teeth wielding, walker scooting mob hit the counters to collect their morning morsels, like a rabid pack of wolves to a carcass in the wilderness. I had to rush and get out of the way or fall victim to the stampede. Janice explained to me that since the last cook had left three weeks ago, and she had filled in for lunch and dinner, they had been eating corn flakes and rice puffs each morning. Today they were having eggs, sausage, grits and toast. I would have run too, at their age they probably thought it was their first breakfast after the rapture.

I did like to see the smiles on their faces and their kindness even though they were brainwashed into giving up the normal world and all their money for these fundamentalist freaks. The cottage houses I saw appeared to be no bigger than the room I was staying in. They were referred to by staff as elderly *"saints of God"*. For the most part they were very saintly and sweet.

On occasion, one or two would get cranky if their food was just not exactly the perfect temperature they wanted. When they would complain food was a bit cold, it was very hard not to say, "It would not be cold if Brother Al were not a windbag with a twenty minute blessing, it would still be warm".

That was not so intolerable because I could take my anger for his ministerial need to preach while praying, preach while talking and preaching just to hear himself make noise, on scrubbing pots in hot water in a 120 degree kitchen with nothing but a fan and curse him all morning, then start the noon meal. I would vent while working and smile when anyone else looked on. Then after three meals and three kitchen cleanups, it was near seven at night and I was so tired the only thing I wanted was a bath and my bed. I was even too tired to enjoy the outdoors with no fences.

A few days passed and I was left to handle the kitchen alone since Janice was falling behind on her duties. I did well to manage and actually get the breakfast done by seven am, but I did start that first morning I was to be alone at four am just in case. I managed but every night it was the same routine, go to my room, take a quick bath, put ointment on my chapped hands and blistered feet, then pass out from exhaustion. Good thing Sunday had just two meals, and the late afternoon was to be spent in prayer individually in our rooms, I took that opportunity to sleep and write.

I was just getting adjusted when I noticed Brother Al was always hanging around and watching me. He gave me the creeps. His lurking reminded me of the chills I would get when I saw a spider creeping on a wall. He need to be swatted with a big shoe, and squashed.

Then he kept getting closer and closer, and I remembered Janice's warning a few weeks prior, and kept moving away, then he grabbed me and I was horrified. I don't to this day remember much more than him shoving me to the floor and me waking up later there on that floor with Janice standing over me, bruises on my arms and a knot on my head and so much pain. She said to me, "I am sorry, but you cannot tell anyone or they will say you are trying to destroy the reputation of a man of God". She then told me that is why the last cook left. She helped me to my feet, and to get cleaned up.

I could barely stand, my legs wobbled like broken spindles as I made my way to the bathroom. I felt sick and just wanted to throw up. I was angry. I was not going to let this man get away with this and if I could not tell someone I was going to get even. I would just have to figure out what it is I was going to do. The pain was so bad I took 4 aspirin and struggled to finish cleaning up the supper dishes so I could just go to bed.

Every morning he perched at the head of the same table with a smug look on his face as if he were untouchable. Each time I saw him my anger grew and I knew I had to get him back for what he and every one of these crazy people had been doing to me. Then one day while cleaning under the sink I saw a bottle of ant poison that said flavored and odorless. I saw my opportune moment to get even with the bastard. So in my immature teen mind I planned it out. Since he always sat in the same spot like it was a throne, I would douse his silverware in ant poison containing arsenic and place them on his napkin and make him vomit as he had made me wretch so many times before by his disgusting act of cruelty on me. Then I did it.

I look back and think now, that was not such a smart move, because he got very ill, almost died and I did read in the Bible you do go to hell for murder. That same week they had figured out what I had done. I surely thought they would call the police and I would go to jail and that would be a relief in comparison to this. I was wrong and I guess the reason they did not call the police is because they knew the secrets that these fundamentalist group nuts had for fondling and raping young girls would be found out. Instead I was sent straight back to the main compound to once again for the third time reside in a reform home within the grounds to 'remove Satan and find God'.

I did try to explain why I did it, but nobody would listen, not even my own mother even let me utter one word in my defense. She turned her back and refused to even speak to me. I felt I was destined to a lifetime of hell on earth.

-14-

Back once again behind barbed wire fences just to be drug by force to another dorm, stripped and have every orifice probed for contraband and placed back into a confinement room to experience the solitude, darkness and twenty-four hours of prayer and preaching via loudspeaker blaring above my head. Damn the luck! I didn't even bother fighting any more. I was still too tired and sore. Back to the toilet tissue earplugs I go. Time went by slowly and I think I slept almost the whole time I was in that dark room all alone. I felt like I was doomed to this life and I would either have to learn to give in and be this robotic person they wanted, or kill myself, but I was too chicken for suicide because I really did believe God would not like that and that one day perhaps the God grandma prayed to and taught me was kind would rescue me before I did try to end my own life.

After seven days I was let out to shower and a two hour lecture on how I was going to go straight to hell because no Christian would harm such a great "Minister of God". It probably was really a good thing I had not eaten the crap they shoved in the door for me that morning or I would have thrown up right then. Minister of God my ass! More like perverted Spawn from some twisted alternate world. I didn't say a word. Why should I? These people were convinced that the leaders in charge walked on water. I would just be another lost soul trying to undermine the will of God.

I was left in the charge of a fellow inmate at the dormitory. I was not allowed to talk to anyone unless it was to ask this "sister leader" for something of importance, or permission to use the bathroom under a close watchful eye. I was still so angry, I might have well just been fed t-n-t and have someone light a match. Either way the end result was going to be an explosion. I just was not sure when the explosion would happen or how long I could contain my anger.

Her chore daily was to wash the linens and things for the staff that resided in the dorms to supervise the girls. I had to go along with her all day and help wash and fold the sheets, towels and blankets in a small hot laundry room with no air conditioning in Texas in the summer. Oh it was sheer misery! As each day passed I had to listen not only to preaching and the teachings of the staff and ministers, but the ranting of this girl named Ella who was a junior clone version of all of them. Day in and day out as we folded clothes, cleaned up, ate meals and walked to and from things, she ran her mouth continuously about how I was wicked and needed to repent like she did and find God, and a purpose for my life. All the while, thinking to myself, that my only purpose and mission was to survive her before I choked the life out of her.

Then one afternoon came, I had reached my limit. It was either Ella shut up or I was going to shut her up myself. I wanted to just tear a sheet into a long strip and hang her with it and watch her squirm, like she made my insides crawl as she spewed that brainwashed message over and over. I had yet another moment of weakness and stupidity as I stared up at an old clothes Iron sitting atop a hot water tank. Ah I could just reach fast, grab it and knock her over the head and make a run for it.

What the hell was I thinking when I found it in my hand and covered in blood! I had grabbed it, swung and sent her crashing to the floor. She laid there with her forehead split wide open and blood spilling everywhere? I ran. Rushing from room to room and down halls, I tried so desperately to find a door to get out of and just run until I could run no more, and found none. I felt like a pig in a maze of fencing trying to escape slaughter. I started to cry, and panic, and ran to the laundry room and tried to break the window glass on the nailed shut window, then the 'God Police' got me. Surely there was hell to pay.

After several hours of screaming and being told I was an attempted murderer, I screamed "yes and I would do it again, and I would kill all of you". That did not go over well. The room fell dead silent for a minute, and then all hell broke loose. Kicking and screaming I was stripped again, in the presence of a few dozen women and men, they proceeded to slap me, spit on me and tell me that I was blasphemous and needed punishment. So what the hell did they think they were doing for the past few years? They drug me to an office in the front of the dormitory, and bent me over a table and proceeded to paddle the demons out of me until I wished I would just pass out. I was then drug away. My eyes too swollen to see where I was heading and hurting too much to care and content with just knowing the beating had stopped. They threw me onto a mattress and I heard a door slam behind me. I woke up back in the dark confinement *hole*, naked and butt so swollen I could not even bend my legs for fear of my skin splitting.

I cried and begged God to just let me live long enough to once again play the game and get out of there before I killed someone or myself. I do not remember for sure how long I stayed in there, but I remember writing a poem and memorizing it because I felt at that time, I would die there and never have a chance to see the outside world again. My will at that time was broken. I had to give in and be what they wanted me to be or die. In tear-filled moments of darkness I pleaded repeating my poem over and over to God begging for either relief or death.

One more day Dear God I plead

To Your good book I promise heed.

I cannot take this awful pain

Being myself there is no gain

I come to you with open arms

Please help me avoid their willful harm

I cannot do this all alone

My will and spirit now are gone

I know you hear me and listen well

Help me survive this earthly hell

I know you not as they have taught

For people like me your forgiveness sought

Let me free and you will see

The simplicity of my loyalty.

I know I can do this me and you

Please show me what I need to do.

I know that day the real God heard me, because I did heal, I did get out of the hole, and I eventually did surrender my will long enough to play the game well. I played it well enough to survive until I was released from the reform dormitory, put back into my mother's trailer on the compound and we left there to start again in Missouri. To this day, spiritual in nature I truly believe the God I hold reverent is not the same God they wanted me to believe in. Because the God I prayed to finally heard me.

You may be shocked, riveted, appalled or shake your head in disbelief, but to this day Fundamentalist Extremist groups do exist and mislead thousands into believing nothing but good happens behind their sacred walls, but I lived behind them and bear the scars upon my soul that will remain healing decades later, while some like my friend Terry, who meant so much to me while we were together there, was so torn and confused, she ended her life six months after leaving to stop her emotional suffering.

Now many years later, people wonder why some days I am an angry individual inside... I just reply. "I am some days what people made me, on the other days I am the person I am trying to become as I clear the past from my mind. Some days I walk the fence because it's hard to forget when you cannot bring yourself to forgive.

To everything there is a season, and a time to every purpose under the heaven:

A time to be born, and a time to die; a time to plant, and a time to pluck up that which is planted;

A time to kill, and a time to heal; a time to break down, and a time to build up;

A time to weep, and a time to laugh; a time to mourn, and a time to dance;

A time to cast away stones, and a time to gather stones together; a time to embrace, and a time to refrain from embracing;

A time to get, and a time to lose; a time to keep, and a time to cast away;

A time to rend, and a time to sew; a time to keep silence, and a time to speak;

A time to love, and a time to hate; a time of war, and a time of peace.

~ Ecclesiastes 3:1-8 KJV~

They too will have their time to answer for their actions.

9448464R2011

Made in the USA
Charleston, SC
13 September 2011